Empire

of

Beasts

Lost Boys Press

Copyright © 2023
All rights reserved.
ISBN: 997-9-83972913-2-3
First Print Edition – 2023
Cover Design and Edited by
Dewi Hargreaves
www.lostboyspress.com

Foreword

In Empire of Beasts, I am happy to present an anthology that pushes the edge of the conventional. Within you will find beings who live on the peripheries and in the dark corners where others would prefer not to look; this is, as we hoped it would be when we first conceived this book, a collection of alien cultures and thought, perhaps dark and uncomfortable at times—but ultimately, I hope, a satisfying read that makes you ask questions and which sticks with you after you turn the final page.

I would like to offer a tremendous thank you to the reading team who helped to read many, many submissions, and to all the authors who submitted their work to us—it is a great privilege to be trusted as the custodians of these stories, and it was a joy to work with you all.

I hope you enjoy reading this anthology as much as we loved putting it together. Keep your wits about you, for you are now in the empire of the beasts.

Dewi Hargreaves, Editor

Table of Contents

Pilgrimage of the Amalgamal

Quill Holland

"What's that?"

Camara turned around to find her student's gaze fixed intently upon her. The childlike innocence that radiated from his mature body was jarring, and Camara knew it'd take some getting used to. Still, she couldn't blame Derris for his naivety—he was only born yesterday.

"What's what, Derris?"

"What's that?" Derris repeated, pointing at a glass jar filled with greenery that sat atop a bookshelf in the living room.

"That is a closed terrarium. It's a sealed environment, and everything that lives inside it must do so in harmony, otherwise, everything inside will die."

Derris thought about this for a moment. "So, you don't need to feed it? Or water it? How does that work?"

"Well, all the raw materials, like air, water, soil, bacteria, plants, and animals, are placed inside at the beginning of the terrarium's life, and then it's sealed up. A cycle forms within the terrarium: the soil provides nutrients for the plants as they grow, and when they die, they return the nutrients to the soil. Water is the same: both the plants and soil in the terrarium release moisture and water vapor, which condenses against the walls of the terrarium and falls back into the soil to be used again."

Derris's eyes widened. "That's how the Pilgrimage works, right?"

"Basically, yeah. The ship only got one opportunity to accept input into the system. After that, it was sealed up, and set off towards the interstellar medium. Since then, the ecosystem has had to function with the resources it's got—there's no additional input and there's no output. Everything must be reused, recycled."

"Even us?"

"Yes! When we die, we return to the Life Giver. It provides us with the nutrients to develop, grow, and be fed throughout our lives. When we die, our bodies are returned to the Life Giver so the borrowed nutrients can be recycled, feeding the next generation."

"Whoa...that's kinda cool!"

"Yes. Yes, it is."

With his curiosity satiated, at least for the time being, Derris wandered off, seemingly satisfied with the answers he'd been given. As Camara watched him disappear, she smiled. In her mind, the memory of her own experience of this day felt as if it had happened yesterday, and yet twenty-five years had passed. Just like Derris, she had been born into a fully grown body with a young and immature mind.

Camara's first thoughts were of being warm and safe in a quiet and dark place. Suddenly, she was unceremoniously birthed, descending briefly onto the cold, hard floor beneath the artificial womb in which she had grown. Her first thoughts were quickly followed by uncertainty and fear of her new surroundings—the cold floor beneath her and a mechanical hum that filled the air.

Born as all inhabitants of the Pilgrimage were into adult bodies, her mind was prepopulated with a foundational set of knowledge, appearing as thoughts that would bubble up from her subconscious.

You need to breathe, appeared one such thought. Camara gasped, drawing air into her lungs, shocked at first by how cold it was, and then relishing how refreshing it felt.

She felt around in the darkness, trying to make sense of her surroundings. An endeavour complicated by the fact that she was both covered by and sitting in rapidly cooling birthing fluid still dripping down the artificial womb that hung above her. She shivered as the fluid continued to cool.

You need to open your eyes.

Camara opened her eyes and, at first, saw nothing—the world around her was still dark. Then, slowly, her eyes began to adjust. She could see the womb hanging above her, fluid still dripping from its split underside. She cast her eyes around the room, discovering that it was small, cylindrical, and she was in the middle of it. The walls were clad with featureless black panels, except for one segment, which held a mirror instead.

Planting her hands on the ground, she steadied herself before rising to her feet and taking her first shaky steps towards the mirror. Arriving before its reflective surface, a light in the ceiling switched on, illuminating her fully in bright, glaring detail and forcing her to cover her eyes. After a few moments, her sight adjusted to the brightness, and she turned her gaze towards the mirror.

She was covered in feathers. White feathers with dark-brown horizontal bands covered her torso and legs above the knee, and pure white feathers circled around her neck. Beneath the knees, her powerful legs were covered in yellow scales, ending in large, taloned feet. The feathers around her head were dark bluish-grey, whilst lighter feathers adorned her back and wings. Bright yellow circles of skin surrounded her eyes, and a yellow beak protruded from her face.

"What..." she croaked, clearing her throat before trying again. "What am I?"

"You are an Amalgamal," replied a deep, wise voice, whose presence filled the room.

Camara spun around as if expecting some creature to be standing behind her, but the room was empty.

"Who are you?" she demanded of the disembodied voice.

"I am the Life Giver."

Life Giver? Camara understood each word on its own, thanks to her foundational knowledge, but together? This thing gave life? Had it given her life?

"What are you?" she asked.

"I am an artificial intelligence, the mind and soul of the mighty generation ship, *Pilgrimage*."

An artificial intelligence? A generation ship? The *Pilgrimage*? So many new words and new questions flooded Camara's brain. What had it called her before? An Amalgamal? If this...Life Giver had made her, she wondered, was she like it? A thinking computer?

9

"You called me an Amalgamal. You said you give life. Does that mean I am like you? An intelligent machine?"

"No," the Life Giver replied, emitting a sound that Camara could've sworn was a chuckle. "You are alive, a biological child of Earth, an amalgamation of several species, although primarily two; thus, you are classified as a Homo Peregrinus."

Camara's young mind moved quickly, rapidly digesting and distilling the information. The Life Giver had inferred that they were aboard a ship and now stated that she was a child of Earth.

"If I am a child of Earth, why is this not Earth?" She asked. "What is the *Pilgrimage*, and why am I on it?"

"You are a curious one, aren't you? Luckily, you have some time," the Life Giver said. "Earth is—"

The A.I. paused abruptly and remained silent.

"Earth is what?" Camara prompted.

"Earth i-i-i-i-i-i-i-i-i-i-i-i-i-i-i-i-s," the Life Giver said, its voice distorting as if playing a corrupted audio file.

There was another pause, and then it continued.

"The *Pilgrimage* is a generation ship, a self-sustaining terrarium, carrying the heritage of one world so that it might become the genesis of another. She is travelling across the interstellar medium, always moving forwards, steady and unceasing, towards the promised land, a new home."

Camara frowned. "Okay, but what about Earth?"

"Enough questions—it is time for you to go," the A.I. said.

"But you didn't answer my—" Camara began to insist, but the Life Giver cut her query short.

"It is time for you to go," it repeated.

"But there's so much more I want to know!" Camara protested.

"Follow the lights, and they'll lead you to the world and your new life."

Camara wanted to argue further but there was a tone to the Life Giver's voice that said this was not a request. It was an order. Camara turned and found that lights had appeared on the ground, forming a breadcrumb trail of light leading out of the room through a previously unseen passageway.

Doing as she had been bid, Camara followed the path of illumination into the dark. As she shuffled forward, she became aware of other footsteps, of other bodies, shuffling along beside her, a group collectively walking towards an unknown future.

Suddenly the darkness vanished and light flooded into the hallway. Camara and all those around her simultaneously cowered, shielding their eyes from the light. One by one, their visions adjusted, and they began to peer at the end of the hallway and the large hall that lay beyond. Camara looked too, seeing that the hall was filled with individuals of all sizes and shapes, of different colours and faces. She didn't know who they were, but she also knew there was only one way to find out. She walked forward, out of the darkness and into the light.

The entire Amalgamal population of the *Pilgrimage* was gathered in the hall that Camara stepped into. They'd been drawn there by a hardwired instinct, a call to attend the Birthing Ceremony, the day when the Life Giver brings a new generation of Amalgamal into the world.

As the first new Earth child stepped into the hall, a Homo Syndactylus would announce, as was customary, the opening words of the ceremony.

"The Life Giver has created new Earth children! Ring the bells!" the announcer called out, his throat sac inflated, projecting his booming voice easily across the great hall.

As bells began to ring throughout the ship, a choir of Homo Syndactylus started singing the song of renewal, welcoming the new Amalgamal as they emerged from the darkness: the fury and aquatic Homo Ornithorhynchus and flying Homo Pteropus, venomous Homo Ophiophagus, and the green Homo Sphodromantis.

Amalgamal naturally gravitate towards their own type. As Camara stepped into the hall, she scanned the room with her powerful vision, searching for an Amalgamal that looked like her. Her gaze fell upon an older male Peregrinus and she walked towards him, passing through the crowd with ease and grace.

Camara came to a stop before the male and he smiled.

"Hello, young one," he said. "My name is Basir. What is yours?"

11

Camara furrowed her brow, unsure of what her name was, but thankfully a name was another piece of knowledge bestowed upon the Amalgamal by the Life Giver.

Your name is Camara.

"Ah...I think my name is Camara," she said.

"It's lovely to meet you, Camara. Come, let us walk and talk—I can feel you've many questions!"

As the air blew past Camara's face, she smiled wistfully, feeling sentimental for those first days she'd spent with Basir, learning what it meant to be a Peregrinus on the *Pilgrimage*.

"This is incredible!" Derris yelled as he soared past Camara.

His sudden pass was a reminder that it was Camara's turn to teach, passing on to her student the lessons of what this life entailed.

"Watch out for the—" Camara called after Derris as he flew between a pair of Homo Tyto.

"Watch it!" the young Tyto cried out.

"Sorry, Sonya!" Camara said as she flew past.

Derris looped through the air so that he fell in line with Camara, slowing down his speed to remain level. "This has to be one of the best roles on the ship!" he exclaimed.

"It's certainly a fast life! But remember, this is no joy ride—we've got a job to do!"

"Oh yeah, sorry. Flying is just so fun!"

"Yes, it is. But now I want you to focus. Let your body soar; your instincts know what to do. With your autopilot engaged, focus your eyes on the ship below. Scan everything, left to right, back and forth."

"What am I looking for?"

"Anything out of place. A cracked pipe, a torn wire, a fractured support beam. Perhaps an injured Amalgamal or one dealing in criminal pursuits."

"We look out for Amalgamals too? I thought we only checked the mechanical systems."

Camara smiled, remembering a very similar question she'd once asked Basir.

"Therein lies another lesson! We are part of the mechanical system; we're just organic components!" Camara said, paraphrasing Basir's words from what felt like a lifetime ago.

"How does that work?" Derris asked.

"You know the terrarium back at the house?"

"Yeah?"

"Do you remember how I explained that it's a closed system? And therefore, everything within the system needs to be reused and recycled?"

"I remember."

"Well, because of that, everything here exists within a carefully considered and finely tuned cycle, playing on repeat. Too much or too little of something could cause the system to break down, or worse, collapse! That's why every Amalgamal that the Life Giver births has a purpose. We're organic components within the mechanical systems of the *Pilgrimage*."

"Is that why we can't reproduce? To keep the system...tuned?"

"Yes. That's also why our lives are shortened. The system needs the best components, the freshest parts that are best suited to doing what is required."

"That doesn't seem fair. Our ancestors lived long lives and raised families. But we aren't worthy of such simple pleasures?"

"It's all part of the cycle. And look, I know the cycle is..." Camara paused, thinking how best to phrase her words. "The cycle isn't perfect. It demands sacrifice. A multigenerational sacrifice. But one day it'll pay off when we reach our inevitable destiny. When our kin stand upon the soil of the promised land, this way of living will have been worth it!"

Derris nodded. "But why thirty years? It just seems so short," he asked.

Camara hesitated. Privately, she sometimes wished that the cycle was longer than thirty years too, if only so that she could dream a bit longer of the empires that there had once been and of the empires that there would be once again. At least, that's what Camara assumed. Who else other than an empire would build something like the *Pilgrimage*? A mighty vessel capable of sustaining life and carrying it between star systems, traversing the interstellar medium as it did so.

"Do not fear the rhythm of our ways, Derris," Camara said, hoping to soothe his doubts. "I know it can feel daunting, but we must be like a mighty river: steady, unceasing, and focused. We cannot see the ocean, but we know it lies ahead. Never lose sight of the promised land, and you will always have hope!"

"I'll try to remember that."

"Good lad. Now focus on the task at hand."

They continued to soar down the ship's length for some time, keeping their eyes trained on the world passing by beneath them. When they reached the end, they'd land, report any findings, eat, drink, and retake flight, making another pass of the *Pilgrimage*. This was their duty, to soar back and forth—day in, day out—the first line of defence against entropy.

"I think I've spotted something," Derris said cautiously.

"What do you see and where?"

"I believe it's a split coolant pipe in sector 24D."

Camara turned her gaze, focusing on the sector Derris had indicated. Sure enough, there was a pool of coolant on the floor of a utility hallway and a dripping coolant pipe nearby.

"Great spotting, Derris! Let's land and take a closer look."

They dived in unison, quickly accelerating, faster than they needed to, but both enjoyed the exhilaration of the dive and rarely passed on the opportunity to feel the rush. Pulling out of their descent, they landed gently beside the coolant pool.

"What do we do now?" Derris asked.

"We always check for danger first—is there any immediate threat to ourselves, others, or the ship?"

Derris looked around, watched the dripping pipe for a minute, and then said, "I think we're okay—the coolant is only harmful to us if it causes irritation on contact or if we ingest it."

"Good. Next, we consider temporary remediation. Is there anything we can do here and now to lessen or stop the impact of the issue?"

As Derris again pondered the situation, Camara remembered the first issue she'd encountered—an exploded capacitor—and how Basir had watched and waited while she'd tried to solve the situation.

"Focus on what we can do, Derris—we don't need to architect a complete repair," Camara said, encouraging her student.

Derris nodded. "I believe we should shut off this coolant pipe for now—we can't safely tape up the leak without exposing ourselves to the coolant, and we don't want to keep wasting it either."

"Very good. On which side of the pipe should we close off the flow?"

"This is a cold coolant pipe, so the fluid is running towards the radiators at the stern of the ship, so we should close the flow at the closest bow side flow limiter."

"Well done! You're a quick study Derris," Camara said, walking over to the nearest flow limiter and turning the dial until the pipe was closed. "Now, what do we do to finish up?"

"We write a report and figure out whom to report the fault to, which would be the Homo Castor, right?"

"Spot on! Let's get this report written and delivered so we can get out of here—I hate the smell of coolant."

Time and tide wait for no Amalgamal, or so the saying goes. As the years started to fly past quicker and quicker, Camara found herself recalling the past more and more. Memories of her days with Basir, all the mistakes and lessons she'd had along the way—lessons she was now teaching Derris, and mistakes she was helping him avoid, all whilst he managed to stumble into entirely new ones.

Camara was also painfully aware of the ever-present timer in her life, of the cycle and its motions, ceaselessly marching on. Those thoughts and memories had a way of finding Camara when she least expected it: at night just as she was about to fall asleep or in the mornings when Derris made them both breakfast—any time her mind had a few moments of rest, really. As Camara watched Derris applying an emergency solder to a severed electrical wire, she found her mind wandering into the past.

"Your welds are sloppy today, Camara. Which isn't like you—is there something on your mind?" Basir asked.

"It's nothing," Camara replied, finishing off another poor weld.

"Do you want to try that again, but with a little more truth this time?"

"It's nothing, really!" Camara insisted.

Basir raised an eyebrow and gave Camara an intense, quizzical stare.

"Okay, fine!" Camara snapped. "You said last night you only had a few months left! And that's not fair! I don't want you to go! Why do we have to be on this stupid ship doing these stupid repairs?"

"It's all part of the cycle, Camara."

"Don't lecture me with the cycle bullshit again!"

Basir's shoulders fell and he bowed his head, as if the weight of the *Pilgrimage* suddenly rested upon his shoulders. He sat down clumsily, almost stumbled really, and buried his face into his feathers.

Camara took a step forward, shocked by her mentor's change of demeanour. "Sorry...I didn't mean...I didn't mean to hurt you."

Basir raised his head slightly. "The *Pilgrimage* cannot make its journey without us, and we cannot make the journey without it. We are inseparably bound to one another; our society is built upon this cycle of servitude to each other—it is a symbiosis we cannot live without," Basir said quietly. "If I have failed to teach this to you, then I have failed the Pilgrimage itself. Your discontent, left unchecked and unresolved, threatens the balance of our way of life."

Camara sat down beside Basir. "I wasn't trying to cause trouble. I...I'm afraid of being here without you. And I don't understand why you must go, is all."

"The *Pilgrimage* exists in a state of repetition. Everything, as you know, is reused and recycled in a carefully considered and finely tuned cycle. Too much or too little of something and the system can break down or collapse. That's part of why our lives are short—too many of us, and there'd be too high a demand on the ship's resources. Too few of us, and the ship would be unable to address all its maintenance requirements."

"But—" Camara tried to interject, but Basir cut her off.

"Let me finish, Camara—please."

Camara nodded.

"Sure, it'd be nice to live long lives with large families. But the *Pilgrimage* wasn't built for that. It was built to cross the interstellar medium and deliver us to the promised land. Now, that is no easy task. In fact, it's a task that demands a multigenerational sacrifice. We may not reap what we sow, but our kin will, one day. And by the Life Giver, they will be grateful for our sacrifice."

"But you'll be gone soon! And I'll be alone for twenty years! I don't know if I am ready for all of that!" Camara insisted, tears spilling over and running down the length of her beak.

"Don't be sad, Camara. Time does not feel sad for us as we step out of its waters, so why should we be miserable that it has brought us to the point of disembarkment?" Basir said, tapping into a hidden well of positivity, for both his sake and that of his student. "How many creatures do you think are in the universe that can say they lived a life aboard a generation ship? We are interstellar beings, a title not to be taken lightly!"

Camara sniffed, wiped away some tears, and made a weak attempt at a smile.

"I know you don't feel ready. Hell, I didn't feel ready when my teacher neared the end of her cycle," Basir continued.

"You didn't?"

"Not in the slightest. But do you know what they said to me?"

Camara shook her head.

"She told me that it wasn't a question of whether we are ready or not, as most of us hardly ever are ready for the challenges we are confronted by; such is life. The question is how are we going to respond to the challenges that arise?"

Basir turned towards Camara, reaching out and placing his wings around her shoulders, turning her so she faced him.

"Look at me. Do we run from challenges?" Basir asked.

"No," Camara whispered.

"I couldn't hear you, Camara. I said, do we run from challenges?"

"No!"

"Do we cower before them?"

"No!"

"Then what do we do?"

"We stand and face them!"

"Exactly! We stand, and we face them!"

"Does this look correct?"

Derris's voice broke through into Camara's thoughts, snapping her out of the past.

"S-s-sorry, what?"

"I was asking if this looks correct?" Derris repeated, pointing towards the soldered electrical wire.

Camara looked at her student's handiwork and smiled. "Yes, that looks really good!"

"Thank you—ah, you seemed...distant. Is everything okay? Anything on your mind?" Derris asked.

"It's nothing," Camara replied.

Derris didn't press further, and the pair saw out the rest of the day in silence. But as the evening rolled around, they gathered before the fireplace in their home, as was the habit, and Camara would usually share a story with Derris.

"What stories do you have for me tonight?" Derris asked, breaking the silence that had persisted since their afternoon conversation.

Camara sighed. "I'm not sure—I feel as if I have told you most of my stories by now."

"Well, you have been telling them for four and a half years!" Derris chuckled.

Camara simply nodded. It really had been four and a half years already, hadn't it? It had felt like forever, yet it was really no time, she mused.

"I wasn't honest with you earlier, and for that, I apologise," Camara said.

"I know," Derris replied. "Do you want to talk about what was really going on?"

"Not really...but I think I need to. I was lost in a memory earlier when you were soldering. Thinking back to a day a lot like this, probably around the same time too. Basir and I had argued because I was upset, aware that his cycle would end soon."

"Did you stay angry at each other?"

18

"No. We wrapped up the argument out in the ship, but once we'd gotten home and sat down, as we are now, he looked at me with a sad, knowing gaze and said, 'Camara, the trouble with life is you think you have time.'"

Derris furrowed his brow. "What did he mean by that?"

"Well, he went on to explain that the twenty years that lay before me—the twenty years that I was fretting about—they'd pass all too quickly. And in the future, when I looked back upon those years, I'd realise how short they'd actually been. The anguish I'd felt at the time, stemmed from…a fear, I guess, a fear that I'd be alone for a long time… because I thought I had a lot of time ahead of me."

Derris smiled. "Basir had another lesson for you though, didn't he?"

Camara smiled too. "Yes, he did. He reminded me that I wouldn't be alone; that Sonya the Tyto lived next door, and Malcolm the Lupis lived across the way, and that they were but two examples of the kin I shared the ship with. And so long as we all had each other, we would never be lonely. He told me twenty years would fly by and before I knew it, I'd have a student of my own. A young Amalgamal that would look to me for guidance and knowledge, just as I had looked to him for all these years."

Camara paused, taking a moment to wipe away a few tears that had welled up and made themselves at home upon her beak.

"There will be times ahead, when you are faced with challenges, and I won't be there for you to turn to. So instead, you must look those challenges in the eye and say, 'Not today. You shall not best me. I am an Amalgamal of the generation ship, *Pilgrimage*. It is my duty to serve the journey, to sustain its passage through the interstellar medium, so that one day…'"

"One day, our kin might stand upon the soil of a new world, the living legacies of Earth, flourishing under the watchful eye of the Life Giver," Derris finished the sentence.

"Exactly. I wish I could be here for longer, serving the *Pilgrimage* alongside you, but the cycle continues. The baton shall pass in a few months, and you shall serve the ship beside your kin."

"I know," Derris said. "And I shall remember this. It shall be the final story I tell my student one day. The tale of how Camara taught me not to be sad but to take joy in the journey and to trust the cycle."

Camara smiled. "That sounds like a good story to tell."

A river always flows forwards. Its currents ebb and flow, but they do not stop, nor do they turn back; they always continue inexorably onwards, towards the ocean, towards its destiny. So too does the mighty generation ship, *Pilgrimage*, move forward, going through the motions of its internal cycle, like a heartbeat, keeping the ship and its purpose alive.

It was those internal rhythms that sprung into action once again, issuing a biological summons, calling the Amalgamal forth to gather in the hall of the Life Giver. The difference was that it would take life instead of giving it this time.

The usually open space of the hall had been filled with steel gurneys which arose from the floor, one for each member of the old Amalgamal generation. It was quite a sight to behold, the assortment of individuals shuffling into the room: some covered in feathers, some covered in fur, and others still covered with scales instead. Everyone entered the hall in pairs, comprised of a student and a teacher, making their way towards the nearest vacant gurney.

"How are you feeling?" Derris asked, as he helped Camara onto the cold surface of a gurney.

"Okay," Camara replied as she lay back for what would be the last time. "It'd be nice if these things were heated, but I suppose that won't matter for much longer."

Derris smiled for a brief moment.

When Camara had been in his shoes, twenty-five years ago as a student herself, Basir had also used humour to make light of the situation. He'd explained it as being something of a coping mechanism.

A choir of Homo Syndactylus began to sing the song of passing, their voices filling the hall with a sombre and yet comforting sound. It was a reminder that time was running out, that the cycle was coming to its end. Now was the time to say any final words.

As Derris looked down at Camara and she up at him, they both smiled, remembering their time together. From the moment Derris had stepped out of the Life Giver, to their first flight together, to the countless days spent patrolling back and forth across the ship and the nights afterwards telling tales in the dark—it'd all been quite the ride, short and sweet.

Camara chuckled.

"What is it?" Derris asked.

"I just had a thought. How strange of a juxtaposition it is, for time to be so fleeting and yet...so endless."

"When you say it like that, it all seems so simple, but when I turn it over in my head, it all feels so complex."

Camara nodded. "Perhaps time is not meant to be understood, at least not in any great detail. Maybe it is only meant to be experienced."

The choir's symphony was rising, and Camara could feel her time slipping away, painfully aware of the second-hand tick, tick, ticking. She looked at Derris, wanting to tell him how proud she was of the student he had been and of the teacher he would become. But she couldn't speak. Camara's mouth had run dry. She'd waited too long, and now couldn't say her final piece.

The end was too near, the cycle on the verge of repeating. This was the nature of their world, of their way of life aboard the *Pilgrimage*. But oh, how Camara wished it wasn't, if only to have five more minutes of speech. Yet, even if she had wanted to fight the ship's currents, to do so was to try and stand one's ground against a river, a task that might seem achievable in the short term but is ultimately an attempt at the impossible. Any duration for which one stands their ground is but an illusion; it will always dispel one's fallacy in due course.

Camara looked at Derris and managed to smile one last time. This was destiny fulfilled, an inevitable fate reaching its conclusion. Sooner or later, you realise you cannot hold back time, nor can you allow it to pass around you, for it is a ceaseless flow that continues onwards; it does not stop, nor does it turn back.

"What's that?"

Derris turned around to find his student's gaze fixed intently upon him. The childlike innocence that radiated from her mature body was jarring, and Derris knew it'd take some getting used to. Still, he couldn't blame her for her naivety—she was only born yesterday.

Derris shifted his gaze, turning in the direction of his student's outstretched wing pointing towards a familiar glass jar that sat atop a bookshelf in the living room, its green insides glistening.

"That is a closed terrarium. It's a sealed environment, and everything that lives within it must do so in harmony, else everything inside will die."

The Blind Forest

Kay Koel

The world began blind. All things did. But the myths said the world would end in blindness as well. And according to Cap, that was a rapidly nearing problem.

Jungle suspected Cap had resolved himself far too early on that fact, though. The purple hued frog lifted his head in the murky darkness surrounding him and blinked. They had reached the edge of the moss-covered tundra that Jungle's kindred frogs—his pod, as they knew them—called home. Jungle set his gaze beyond the mossy flatlands and toward the descending cliffs of the ancient mountain.

"Cap?" Jungle asked. "How long, again, did you say we have?"

Tendrils shivered against Jungle's back. Cap, the short, stocky Psichi mushroom Jungle had recently bonded with, whispered back a reply.

"I don't know." Cap was curt and sharp. "We need to go! He's the last one."

"Could be a she," Jungle murmured and hopped toward the path that wound around the knobby hills that would follow their descent down.

They were not really hills. This was not truly a mountain. It was, and it wasn't. Here in the murky lake, the only mountains were the carcasses of large ancient frogs whose spirits had long left them. The unfortunate many who never ascended.

No frog had ascended since the darkness fell. Perhaps long before that. Jungle had heard all the myths. The rites of ascension and the paths to the celestial realm had all been lost.

But Cap said he knew where they were. In fact, the young fungi was rather adamant about that, despite the many visions other prophetic fungi had granted. For all the prophets, no fungi had found a path yet, though. So Jungle had to hedge his bets on Cap.

This was, after all, why the young fungi now rode on the junior frog's back.

Cap's snippy voice brought Jungle back to the world around him. "I don't care, he or she, we don't have time to argue. Please, hurry!"

Jungle hopped on, forward along the path. "How do you know about this great frog anyway?" he asked.

"Rumors follow roots," Cap retorted. "Even frog rumors. Fungi like to talk. The elders especially."

"You're starting to sound like an elder," Jungle sighed. He picked out a bend in the path and followed it. They were off to find the ancient frog. The last frog who remembered the sun.

Jungle wondered how old a frog had to be to remember the sun. Darkness prevailed here in the misty lake. It covered even the tops of the very mountains themselves.

"All adolescent fungi do is listen," Cap complained. "They listen all day and can't do anything until they get chosen. Thank the sun's rays you picked me."

Jungle wasn't sure he was going to be so thankful if this chatter kept up. Cap hadn't stopped chattering. Of course, there was quiet during the rite of choosing. There was always quiet.

The rites came twice a year. Frogs would migrate from the pools in the mountains and follow the trails to the tribes of the fungi. Every pod had their own trails, and their own deals with the fungi, but for the most part Jungle was certain all pods had the same tradition of migration and choosing.

It had finally been Jungle's year. Three floods and Jungle was old enough to choose a bondmate. No easy task for any frog. After all, the fungi were a revered and respected kind, but you didn't want to bond with someone you couldn't tolerate. Worse, no frog wanted a fungi who couldn't give dreams and visions. Thankfully, the Psichi fungi were a system revered for their visions.

Cap hadn't given Jungle a single vision, though, only talk. His many-spotted mushroom cap had caught Jungle's eye. The elders had warned Jungle to be wary of choosing on appearances.

24

"Hurry," Cap went on.

Jungle groaned and stopped hopping in the middle of the trail. "It will be at least a hundred hops to the next pool, Cap, can I please have some silence?"

"You're the one asking questions."

Jungle silenced himself and hopped off. Above himself, though, Jungle caught Cap whistling through his frills an ancient frog tune. The fungi truly did listen. Perhaps too much.

Jungle hopped on. Only ninety hops to go. The next pool was one the elders had warned him about. The Pod of Dressi frogs. Common looking, and often slow, but stout believers that the frogs who died and were entombed as mountains had achieved true ascension. Dressi adhered to the idea that frogs lived on through the fungi who spawned on their backs from the original spore.

The Dressi believed in the end times, though. That all frog kind would be wiped out. The fungi too, and that the world would be consumed by a flood. Jungle remembered learning about them as a tadpole.

The Dressi did not take kindly to those who believed different. Still, they were Jungle and Cap's only chance.

Jungle's elders had sanctioned the journey insofar as they sanctioned all journeys of enlightenment. It wasn't uncommon for a young frog to seek his own prophecy. But Cap's request had been very specific. They needed to see the last frog who remembered the sun. That was the only way to stop the world from ending.

Jungle knew stories about the ancient frog. Myths, mostly. All frogs who survived more than two hundred floods had a few myths to their names. No one knew this frog's name, though, for names were forgotten in exile.

Any frog who grew too large became exiled to the lake. It was on them to find their enlightenment and seek their ascension. None could tread upon their backs, except the Dressi.

That was why Jungle and Cap hopped on, another forty hops, toward the pool of Dressi.

Jungle himself was squeamish at the idea of contact with the great frog given the customs, but the elders had assured him the Dressi would make it possible. They could satiate Cap's desire to speak with the ancient frog without breaking the laws.

"I am beginning to wonder how no one gets sick off of this," Cap moaned.

Jungle slowed. "Off of what?" he asked and rolled his eyes back; though he could not see Cap, he caught a blur of the mushroom's white top.

"This motion," Cap said. "It's positively nauseating."

"You will get used to it," Jungle said and hopped on. "But I will try to be gentle along the way. I guess we're both still getting our legs under us."

"I have roots," Cap retorted.

"Roots," Jungle corrected. He sighed and leaped longer, softer strides. They passed large knobs covered in brown moss. They dripped moisture. Everything in the lake seemed to have a film of wet covering it.

"Cap, what do you know of the mountains in the lake?"

"I know that's where we live."

"Do you know how many there are?"

"No. Do you?"

"I was told there are hundreds, but the elders said more are made every day."

"That's a lot of frogs dying."

Jungle sank into his next hop, deflated. A lot of frogs were dying. They couldn't seem to stop dying. For all the fungi who offered their visions, and for all those that eased pain, it did seem rather pointless.

"That's why we're going to find the sun, right?" Jungle asked.

"We're going to capture the sun, and the world will keep going," Cap corrected. "Maybe then less frogs will die."

"I heard the sun is in the same plane that frogs ascend to."

Cap shivered, probably shaking his domed head. "No, the sun is a big burning ball in the sky that used to be held by a ring of mushrooms. I'm going to bring it back to them. We'll hold the sun again!"

Jungle wondered how Cap knew what the sun looked like, given that all fungi were blind. Perhaps, like everything else, it was because Cap had heard it from someone.

"Well it's probably a good thing either way," Jungle said. He could see the tall fungi that grew near the entrance of the Dressi pool. The Dressi did not carry fungi; instead they allowed the fungi to grow near the pool and only took them onto their backs before death. A way to harbor their little circle of life.

Jungle hopped past the sentry fungi. He felt Cap's tendrils wrap around him tight.

The sentries seemed to take no notice, though.

Jungle frowned. He had been wondering why none of the other fungi ever spoke to him. Even those who his friends had chosen, even the elder fungi, had all lain silent during the choosing. Perhaps it was cultural, not to speak in the presence of someone you weren't bonded to.

No one else had minded Cap's chatter, though.

Maybe they already knew the fungus was weird. Jungle should have noted that earlier on.

A large frog hopped into Jungle's path as he slowed. The young frog leaped back to avoid a collision and quickly stuck his nose to the ground. "Honored elder," Jungle blurted out. "I'm from the Genrit Pod! Please have compassion and hear me."

That was the correct greeting, right?

"By the ancestors," the old frog bellowed. His body was double Jungle's size already. Not large enough by far to be exiled, but showing his age. "A Genrit," the word came off the old frog's tongue as if it were a stuck fly. "What sends you hopping here?"

Jungle looked up. He licked his eyes twice to show additional respect. "I've come asking a favor."

Cap shuddered with excitement. "Finally!"

The Dressi elder sat back on his haunches and peered down at them. "A favor of what manner?"

"The exiled."

A low rumble, the kind which extends a frog's throat and makes it boastfully bloated, echoed in the Dressi elder's chest. "The exiled, you say. You wish to break your own culture's code, so you come to us."

"Yes."

"No," said the elder. He leaned forward and landed on his forelegs. "We will not."

"But!" Jungle tried to hop after the retreating Dressi. "I thought—"

"—you are a tadpole!" spat back the Dressi, "if you thought we would help a Genrit break his own codes."

Jungle sank back onto all fours. Cap's shuddering stopped.

"He has to help us!" the fungus screeched. It made Jungle's head hurt. "We came all this way!"

"Be quiet," Jungle panted. He inched forward. "Elder," he called and pitifully licked his eyes. "Please. Is there nothing you will do for me?"

The old Dressi turned. His mottled skin turned darker and his eyes closed to slits. There was not enough room for Jungle's tongue on them.

Jungle felt the accusatory disrespect sink in like an unpleasant dryness.

"Which frog do you seek?" the Dressi demanded.

Jungle bowed his whole body. "I don't know his name."

"Tadpole!" The Dressi spat back. "Then how were you going to seek help?"

"Tell him about the sun!" Cap urged.

Jungle shuddered, unsure if that was a good idea. He tried to look up anyway, with wide eyes, hoping the respect of exposing them was enough. "He's the last frog who has seen the sun."

At that, the Dressi elder harrumphed and choked on his own tongue in humor. "You mean to tell me you seek Ruel? The most ancient of frogs? I most certainly will not disturb her."

Jungle leaped back as the Dressi spat out his tongue in an attack at the young frog's eyes. Jungle snapped his eyes shut quickly.

Her?

"We got a name!" Cap rejoiced.

Jungle retreated. He should have known the Dressi would be unhelpful. In every story they always stopped the hero in their tracks.

The old Dressi frog had lumbered off by the time Jungle had opened his eyes.

Jungle sighed. They would need to go around this pool. His skin felt dry at the notion, but it was all they could do.

Jungle rapidly hopped back to the trails and glanced at the sentries. They watched in silence.

"He attacked my eyes," Jungle shivered as he leaped up the mossy knobs and climbed along them in a direction that would take them around the pool. He stopped, though, halfway. "Cap, we don't know where we're going."

"But we have a name!" Cap's moodiness fled in the face of his optimism. His optimism made him chatty.

Jungle sank at the base of a massive knob hill. "What good does that do us if we have no directions?"

"We could ask for directions."

"We just tried! And anyway, we can't—"

"Jungle stand up!" Cap's voice grew urgent. "I feel a tremor."

Jungle reared back up and scrabbled back around the knob. He heard the faint thud of a front set of legs and then a back, and then the recoil of a launch. Another frog was hopping their way.

Should they hide? Should they wait it out?

"Talk to them," Cap urged.

How did the fungus always seem to know what Jungle was thinking?

"I just do," Cap added.

Jungle shook his head, not caring if it made the fungus nauseated. Jungle hopped out around the knob again. A bright green frog came leaping down. Jungle looked up, and realized only too late the frog was landing where Jungle stood.

They both cried out as they collided.

"Cap!" Jungle squirmed free, legs kicking hard. He hoped the fungus hadn't been flattened.

"Alive." Cap's voice swirled dizzily.

Jungle righted himself and came face to face with a frog only a bit larger than him, and far brighter. While Jungle sported the purple hues which blended him into the darkness, this frog was almost phosphorescent, as phosphorescent as anything could be without light. Its green skin shimmered moistly.

"Is it just me or do they look mad?" Cap whispered.

Jungle's eyes widened. He licked them both repeatedly. "I'm sorry!"

The other frog *had* run into him, though.

"Don't think that matters," Cap whispered.

Shut up, Jungle thought.

"Fine."

The other frog looked down on the penitent young bondmates. Then burst out in a croak of laughter. "I thought I flattened you boys!" An eye closed halfway. "You are...boys, or have you not been sexed yet?"

Jungle's tongue stuck stiff to his eye at the horror of the idea of being *sexed* as an adult frog.

29

The elder frog only laughed more. "That one got you, didn't it. Course you're boys, I can see because you got no spots." The frog hopped around. "Unlike me."

She wriggled her shoulders and then turned back around to face the two. Jungle noticed also the flat top of a red mushroom on her back. Below it ropes lashed a fly trap at the frog's side. The jar buzzed full. There were fireflies inside, blinking away.

The elder frog lowered her face so she was level with Jungle. "Well, since you aren't flattened, what's this talk of directions?"

Jungle looked away. "We um, needed directions to..." the words were heavy on his tongue and threatened to loosen it, so it lay useless before him. Or worse, he might swallow the thing.

"We're looking for directions to Ruel!" Cap insisted. "C'mon, say it."

"That!" Jungle's head popped up.

Again, the elder frog closed one eye. "That? Directions to that? And what in the misty lake pray the ancestors tell me, is *that*?"

Jungle blinked. "Um, what Cap said. That is what we need." He backed up an inch or two. This elder frog looked like she might have a long sticky tongue.

"Cap? OH!" Her laughter returned. "You must mean your bond-mate. Of course, of course. You *must* know I can't hear a word he says. Only you can hear his prophecies."

"Me?" Jungle's voice echoed between the knobs they sat between. Somewhere around them, a drop of water fell from a moss tuft. It hit the ground in the silence.

"Yes, only you," repeated the old frog. "Only I can hear Pink back here. Did your elders teach you nothing? What are you? Dendi? Issin? Ahhh oh, no, here's one, Telethar?"

"Genrit."

Her tongue flicked up to one eye. "I'm so sorry."

Jungle sank down and huddled up in self-disdain. "You all keep saying that."

"The Genrit aren't well known for being open minded, you know. And they're recluses. All their young go out for enlightenment and come back half-brained dimwits babbling about visions. It's because they trust too much in those Psichi. They're too strong. It's all acid to the brain, you know."

Jungle felt Cap stiffen. The fungus was repeating obscenities from both frogs and fungi.

And yet the elder frog couldn't hear them. And Jungle couldn't hear any other fungi.

Did this mean...? Cap could only be heard by Jungle, which meant all his words were telepathic. That explained the visions.

The elder frog licked her eyes three times. "I've insulted you enough. Anyway, back to your directions."

"You aren't Dressi," Jungle sighed. "You can't help us."

"Oh, I can't?"

"Well."

"Ruel!" Cap repeated, breaking the string of curses. They picked back up. Jungle couldn't think straight over the young fungus.

The elder frog proved right about one thing. Cap was going to liquefy half Jungle's brain if he kept this up.

"We're looking for an exile frog," Jungle finally admitted as the cursing calmed. "Ruel."

"I knew her," the old frog licked one eye sadly. "You won't find her. She's gone into the lake. I assume you already asked the Dressi to speak on your behalf."

Jungle bobbed his head. Cap bobbed his.

"Well then, they've given their answer. But," the elder frog looked back. "The Dressi are all frogs with their tongues up the wrong end. They don't help anyone despite the stories. That's why they don't care about your laws, because they don't care except about lounging and making up fly's tales."

Jungle nodded.

"What do you wanna know from Ruel anyway?" The elder frog reached back and in one motion took the lid off the jar and caught a firefly. The lid was replaced before another insect could escape.

The firefly vanished into her mouth.

"The sun," Jungle repeated what Cap was hammering into his skull at the same time. "We're trying to find the sun."

"Oh. Hmmmm." The ancient frog bowed down and her eyes widened. At least she trusted them. "Well if you wanna know about the sun, I can take you at least to the base of the mountain near her. Maybe, and you didn't hear this from me, if you get to the peak, she'll talk to you. I remember her telling stories about that thing."

31

"You know where she is?"

"Yes. At least, I think I do. She talked about where she'd go in exile a lot, you know."

Jungle could hear Cap's voice leaping inside his head. It was all excitement, and it was beginning to feel like the headache one gets after drying out. Jungle lowered himself to the ground.

It wasn't wrong to *speak* with an exile if one did not climb their back. Most frogs merely abstained so as not to interrupt enlightenment. But the fate of all future frogs, and their enlightenment, might rest on this.

If Cap was right. So far, Cap was only annoying.

"Will you take us?" Jungle licked both eyes, twice.

The old frog laughed. "What's your name, tadpole?"

"Jungle."

"Inventive. I'm Festa. Good to meet you, Jungle. And Cap?"

"*Yes.*" Cap's tone was hurried.

"Yes," Jungle repeated.

"Well," Festa sighed. "I have hunted all day, so I admit I must rest a bit, but if you will rest with me, I will take you."

Jungle hopped a little closer, hesitant. He eyed the fireflies.

"Are you hungry?" Festa crouched under a mossy patch that covered the knob to their right. The moisture slicked her back.

"A little."

Cap's frustration welled up as his tendrils tightened. "We need to go!"

"I'm tired too," Jungle said. A hundred hops was a great length. They'd traveled further than Jungle had ever gone in his life.

"Ah, the days of bonding." Festa settled by the moss. Jungle slowly crouched beside her, just enough to moisten his skin.

"I miss them," Festa sighed. "We never fight anymore. You don't have to say it all out loud, though."

Jungle looked up at Festa. "I don't?"

"They read your thoughts, you know."

Oh, Jungle thought.

"I don't want to stop." Cap's tendrils became tighter. The hurt pressed into Jungle's skin. He huddled up tight. They needed to rest. They'd get further if they rested.

Please.

"Fine," Cap huffed.

Jungle felt the release. His eyes settled closed. *Thank you.*

Jungle hopped in Festa's shadow down the back of the mountain. They'd gone at least three hundred hops and Jungle's toes were beginning to go sore.

"How much further?" Jungle complained.

Cap had been deceptively quiet all day.

"Ah, I don't know." Festa hopped ahead. This was easier for her, being older and therefore covering more ground in a single hop. Jungle needed five hops just to keep up with her. At least Cap was no longer complaining about getting dizzy.

"Where are we going?" Jungle went on.

Festa lifted her head and then took another hop. "To the pond."

"Pond?"

Festa hopped atop a short knob. "Yes," she said and snapped up a firefly from her jar. "Have you never been to the pond?"

"Not if it's this far away." Jungle scrambled up beside her and reclined on the knob. "I only know the pool where I grew from a tadpole into a frog."

"Ah." Festa shook her great head. "The pool is where all the mountains reside. You might know it as the misty lake, or by other names. Some say the first tadpoles were born into it. Now, it's just a big marsh."

"Why do we need to go there?" Jungle crouched and peered into the darkness. He could smell something rather sour and moist very close by.

Festa hopped down. "To cross to another mountain, of course. We aren't as big as the ancient exiles, so we'll go by lilypad."

Jungle hopped after her. He turned his eyes back far as they would go and wondered at Cap's silence. Did fungi sleep? Or was Cap dizzy again?

"I'm not asleep, and I'm not dizzy," Cap's voice dredged up in the back of Jungle's mind. "I'm thinking."

"About?" Jungle asked.

"Shhhh," Festa hushed him. "Not good manners to talk out loud, remember? Talk in your heads."

Jungle sighed. Festa was nice. She shared her fireflies, and fun myths about the sun. She told them one Ruel had told her about how the sun would mysteriously vanish for hours on end. Some frogs thought an old celestial frog was playing tricks on them.

Festa knew about the celestial frogs too, and sometimes she made jokes, but she reminded Jungle too much of the pod mothers sometimes. And the elders too.

"I'm just wondering what Ruel will say," Cap chattered. "If they've seen the sun, why didn't they catch it and bring it back? Why didn't any of the elders before them?"

I don't know, Jungle thought. He should've known any conversation with Cap would be about the sun. Jungle kept after Festa.

They made it down to where the air was all damp. It sank onto Jungle's skin and settled like a thick blanket of moss. Jungle crept after Festa, who wandered down to where the mountain ended and thick, inky water began. Lilypads sat all around, floating on the water.

Lithe little frogs hopped over them once Jungle looked close enough. His eyes widened. "Pad hoppers," he whispered.

"Yes." Festa neared them. She cleared her great throat. "Excuse me, can we get a ride?"

A tiny green frog peered up at them. He held in his hand a thick stalk. "Ride where?"

Festa pointed her head right. "To the east, please. Far east. Far as you can take us."

"Fee is three flies."

Festa unlatched her jar and set it in front of the tiny frog. "Will that be enough?"

He snapped one out of the jar with his long tongue and contemplated the leftover four. "Hop on."

They all clambered onto the lilypad, which surprisingly held under even Festa's weight. Their pilot pad hopper took the front and began to move the lilypad via the stalk in his fingers.

"I'm Ina," he told them as they slid along the water. "What takes you far east?"

"Oh," Festa smiled coyly. "The sun."

Ina scoffed.

Jungle huddled on his portion of the lilypad. Everyone seemed to scoff at Cap's idea. The elders at least had thought he was noble for going after enlightenment.

Cap shivered in anger on Jungle's back. "Mud frogs," Cap cursed.

That wasn't nice.

"I don't care."

Jungle sighed. The inky water rippled around them.

"Why does everybody think the sun is silly?" Jungle looked up at Festa.

She kept her eyes on the mist overhead, watching for flies. "Not silly," she said. "But the sun is gone. What good is there in bringing it back?"

"Enlightenment?" Jungle offered. "And keeping the world from ending..."

Festa scoffed. "And what good is that to someone of your age? You have your whole life to find enlightenment. If the world was going to end, it would've done so already."

"Do you want enlightenment?"

"I want a big, juicy fly." Festa's tongue snapped out in the air.

Jungle blinked as they passed another mountain. He looked up at it through the mist. It seemed taller from the pond. How were they ever to reach the top in time?

"We're running out of time," Jungle sighed.

"Yes," Cap agreed. "Hurry up."

Jungle couldn't. He watched Ina. The pad hooper took his leisure paddling them away from the mountain. It vanished in a few strokes, though, and Jungle leaned back.

Cap, he wondered. *Do fungi seek enlightenment?*

"No," Cap said firmly. "Fungi seek the sun."

Ina moored them to another stationary lilypad at the base of a great mountain and shaded his little eyes to the mountain. "You wanna go up there?" he asked. "To Dart Mountain?"

Jungle saw Festa's eyes grow wide. "Dart Mountain?" she asked. "Is this the furthest mountain?"

Ina pointed to the left. "No, but that's Ruel. She's still..."

"I know," Festa said. She retreated and turned to Jungle. "Alright, tadpole, time to rethink the plan."

"What?" Cap and Jungle echoed in unison.

Festa shook her head. "No one sets foot on Dart Mountain. And I mean no one. The fungi there will kill you and your bondmate and take you over. Turn you into their slave."

"We don't even send our young there," Ina said.

Jungle looked at him. "What?"

Ina staked his stalk on the lilypad. "All pad hopper young make their own journeys, you know. They have to travel to the furthest mountains and return. Prove they're worthy of the pond. That's how they earn their pads." He gestured to his stalk and pad. "But no pad hopper frog goes to Dart Mountain."

Jungle shuddered

"We have to go!" Cap thundered in Jungle's skull. "We have to talk to Ruel!"

"Can we...avoid the fungi on Dart Mountain?" Jungle asked.

"Nope." Festa sat back and set her lips in a long thin line. "No one avoids them. Dart Mountain is a mountain of pure death."

Jungle frowned. "How?" Any kind of enslaving frog- and fungi-eating mushroom sounded like it would be impossible to bond with. The only mushrooms that grew on a mountain came from the spores of the ancient frog's bondmate. Jungle knew when he died, all of Cap's spores would make the next generation of fungi grow on Jungle's back.

"Dart was mad," Ina said. "Or so the legend says. Thought that it was only by doing the bidding of the fungi that he'd find enlightenment." Ina pointed his stalk. "Notice how small he is. Didn't get far in life, clearly."

Jungle's skin felt dry at the implications.

"Sorry, but we are not risking our brains and lives on that mountain," Festa said. "I suppose your sun seeking will have to wait."

Jungle looked to the left. A larger shadow sat there, still moving with breath. Jungle licked both eyes once.

"We should just climb up there and ask," Cap said firmly. "Who's gonna know?"

"No!" Jungle spat out.

Festa narrowed her eyes at him again.

Jungle shied back. He licked both eyes twice. "Sorry," he said.

Festa shook her head. "What's your fungus's brilliant idea?"

Jungle closed his eyes, just to protect himself as he shied back to the furthest corner of the Lilypad. "Climb...Ruel's...back..."

"Hmph." Festa sat heavy on the Lilypad. "That's against all tradition, tadpole."

"I know."

"I know," Cap added. "And I don't care."

"Maybe there's another way to find the sun," Jungle offered both. "Maybe we don't need to talk to Ruel."

"No!" Cap blurted out.

Ina hopped between the two parties. "You know, for all I care, I just ferry around these pads all day. No one cares if I touch the wrong mountain. We send our young out, and they hop all over everyone's back. Can't find a mountain you haven't visited, even if it's still alive. So if you ask me, I don't think old Ruel would mind too much."

Festa looked away. She licked her right eye, angry. "No. I won't condone it."

"They don't...hate you if you touch them?" Jungle looked up at Ina. "Even if they're alive?"

Ina looked back. "They're exiles. Most of them are lonely. Trust me, the young come back with *stories*."

Jungle felt Cap bristle, hopeful. Jungle's own shoulders hunched. Lonely. It made sense. Enlightenment never sounded like it was meant to be lonely. You were supposed to go and find other frogs who survived, find the living. But everyone here was just waiting for death, no matter what they said.

That had to be lonely.

"Okay," Jungle said. He looked at Ina. "Will you take me to Ruel?"

"I won't stand for this," Festa turned. She leaped off their pad onto another, a stationary lilypad. "I'm staying here."

Ina put his stalk in the water. He turned his back on Festa. "Stay if you will. I'll pick you up later."

"This is a mistake," Festa said. "You know it is."

Jungle faced the darkness before himself, though. "I know," he said. "But the elders sent me to find my path. I'm finding it."

"There she is." Ina planted the lilypad as best he could. Stalks poked up around them from the mist. Jungle tentatively looked up at the knobby back of the living mountain before them. He swallowed and almost took his own tongue down his throat too.

Cap stiffened in awe. "Amazing…"

"Moment of truth," Ina said. "On or off, your choice."

"Go!" Cap cried.

Jungle hesitantly hopped to the edge of the lilypad. He looked back at Ina.

"Thank you for taking me. Do you really think Festa is right, though? Am I doing the wrong thing?"

"Festa's traditional," Ina sighed. "You know what, tadpole, here." Ina held out his stalk. "All pad hoppers who travel this far have more than earned their paddles."

"But I'm not—"

"I don't care," Ina offered the stick again. "Take it. And if you get cast out for all this, well, know you can come back to me."

Jungle took the stick. "Thanks."

Jungle faced the mountain. His heart and throat swelled. This was the moment, the moment to choose.

Closing both eyes, Jungle took a leap.

He landed on a coarse, moist back. The sensation of breath came as the ground swelled and Jungle almost lost his balance.

Cap was practically blooming with excitement. "Let's go! To the top!"

Jungle couldn't even see the top. He looked back at Ina.

"I'm gonna go get your friend and take her home. I'll come back." Ina broke off a fresh stalk from the patches around him. He waved.

Jungle nodded. He faced Ruel's back again. This was wrong.

"But you did it," Cap assured him.

"It was still wrong."

"Only until we prove everyone else wrong," Cap added.

Jungle leaped forward tentatively. The knobs were harder to grasp, given that Ruel was alive and still breathing. But Jungle kept going, panting after several hops.

"I can't do this," Jungle said.

He heard water slosh. Jungle looked back to see Ruel moving in the pond, shifting, ever so slightly.

"Can't do what?" a great voice boomed out.

Jungle started. "I'm sorry!" he licked both eyes, repeatedly, and cowered against Ruel's back.

"Is that...voice?" Ruel boomed out. "I hear someone down there." She tried to turn. More water sloshed, this time up and over Jungle as he clung to her back.

"Stop!" he cried out, shivering and shaking.

Ruel paused. "Oh," she sighed. "You must be on my back."

"Y—Yes," Jungle stammered out.

"She's scary," Cap mumbled. "And making me dizzy."

"I know."

Ruel sat still, breathing even again. "It's been so long since I heard a voice," she sighed. Her back arched forward. "Are you here to talk to me?"

"Yes," Jungle said.

Ruel bowed her head forward. "You'd better get up here, then."

It took over five hundred hops. Jungle counted every single one. Having the stalk to carry didn't help, but it made Jungle feel a sense of pride, a sense of belonging as he carried it.

On the way up, they passed some mushrooms, but they were tiny and no more than early spores. The ecosystem here had yet to grow.

Cap also blabbered the whole way, gloating over being right that Ruel would talk to them. Jungle said nothing until he'd reached the twin peaks that were Ruel's eyes. He paused there at the tip of her head and tried to breathe.

Jungle knew he should have rested sooner.

Ruel sat up again once Jungle was secure on her head, but her moving still made him think he was going to tumble down her back and into the water. Jungle trembled until Ruel was still again.

"So," said the exiled frog. "You came to talk to me. How wonderful. I haven't had anyone in so long."

Jungle looked up at the darkness over him. "We came to ask about the sun," he said. "Other frogs say you've seen it."

"Fungi too!" Cap insisted.

"And fungi," Jungle added.

"Hmmmmm." Ruel's throat expanded with the sound. She sank down a little. "Yes, I've seen the sun. It was brilliant. I thought my very eyes might burn out of their little sockets."

Jungle wasn't sure that qualified for brilliant. Gory, perhaps.

"Do you...know where to find it?" Jungle chanced to ask.

Ruel's head lifted a bit. He heard a smile in her throaty voice. "Of course, it's right there."

Ruel's head turned left. Jungle stared at nothing.

"Where?" he asked.

Ruel sighed. "The sun used to shine right through there. But one day it vanished. An old theologian said something might be blocking it. A punishment for the sins of the frogs."

Jungle lowered his head. The sins of the frogs wasn't a new one to him. No one knew what they were, but everyone assumed the frogs had once done something horrible. And for it, the sun vanished. Maybe Cap was right, and the world was ending.

"The sun was owned by the fungi," Cap interrupted. "It wasn't some frog sin. Someone stole it. We're taking it back!"

"Anyway," Ruel went on, not heeding them. "I saw the sun as a tadpole, and when it vanished, my whole pod was in uproar. So they sent me and some others, you might find their mountains now. We climbed up here and found—"

Jungle held his breath.

"—stone," Ruel said. "Just stone. No sun, only cold hard rocks." She lifted her nose. "That's why I sit here now. I always wondered if maybe there was some way through, to the other side. But I'm far too big now."

Jungle crouched and frowned. "Are you...sure?"

Some frogs' brains could grow addled with years. Maybe Ruel's fungi had melted part of her brain.

"Sure as I am of my own name," Rule said firmly. "See for yourself!

Hop up on my eye. Reach out."

Hesitant, Jungle hopped toward one of the peaks of her eyes and climbed it carefully. Reaching out, Jungle pressed one hand out in the blackness.

Jungle's sticky fingers found exactly what Ruel described. Rock, harder than even the ground on a mountain. There were rocks rumored to be in the misty lake too, but Jungle found the substance strange against his fingertips. It was cold and smooth, but it did not give or move when he pressed on it. It felt lodged, like he sometimes was between his brother and sister frogs when sleeping.

Jungle hopped down. "It's there," he said.

"We have to move it!" Cap's tendrils tightened and loosened and practically vibrated. "Please, please, Jungle!"

"You couldn't move it," Jungle said to Ruel. "Why?"

"It only slipped and slid on our fingers," Ruel said.

Jungle looked at the stalk Ina had given him. Hands might not be any good, but what about something stiffer? Like the stalk?

"What are you thinking?" Cap asked. "What I'm thinking?"

Jungle didn't know what Cap was thinking unless the fungus told him.

"I'll tell you." Cap inhaled. "We need to use the stalk on the stones. Like...a spear!"

They were thinking the same. Jungle nodded. "Ruel, may I sit on your eye?"

"Don't damage it."

Jungle hopped up onto her eye. He lifted the stalk and struck it at the stone. Dust fell. Jungle fought the urge to sneeze and struck the stone again. Something moved.

"Again!" Cap cried.

Jungle swung and something cracked. More dust fell. A thin shower of yellow slipped through. Jungle stared at it. Ruel blinked her other eye and moved.

"Child, that yellow ray. Is that—"

"Sun!" Cap practically yelled. "Jungle, again, again!"

Jungle felt the infectious fervor and began to ram at the rocks with the stalk. More of them cracked and moved until finally a chunk fell out. Ruel recoiled as stones fell from the sky and tumbled down. They crashed and splashed into the water below. His fingers scrabbled for grip as Ruel moved.

The dust and Ruel settled. Jungle slid down her eye.

He looked up, blinded.

"It's warm." Cap shivered under the rays.

"The sun," Ruel breathed.

In a few blinks, Jungle could look out. The burning ball in the sky was indeed warm, and bright. It was also brilliant.

Jungle dropped his stalk. "We did it."

"Quick!" Cap urged. "Grab it so I can take it home!"

Jungle was too busy looking around the sky beyond the sun, and at the ground under his feet. His eyes had adjusted for so long that now they hurt in the glare, but he also could see so much more.

And yet, when he looked up, he saw no frogs in the sky. No floating mountains. Where were the celestials?

"Jungle!" Cap's voice slammed into Jungle's thoughts. "I want to hold the sun!"

Jungle blinked. He stretched out both front legs and tried to reach the blazing orb with his webbed fingers. His eyes closed the closer he reached.

His grasp fell short. The sun was too far away.

"I can't," Jungle said. "I can't touch the sun!"

In a rumble, Ruel laughed. "Oh children," she said. "No, you can't touch the sun. It's much too far away."

"But what about the celestial frogs?" Jungle hopped down and onto the top of her head, looking down desperately.

Ruel shook her great head. "Who knows," she said. "Perhaps they too are further away than we can reach."

Jungle flatted on the top of Ruel's head. He felt Cap too, flat against his back. They hadn't found anything at all.

Ruel's knobby back bristled. "It is good to be warm again," she sighed. Her great body heaved and swelled.

Jungle looked up, his eyes half lidded in dejection.

Ruel turned her whole face to the sun. "Thank you," she said. "You've gone where not even I could."

Jungle looked up. He squinted at the white light. It did feel nice. He wanted to lay here and rest his weary body until he'd soaked up all the sun's warmth. Maybe Ruel was right. They hadn't caught the sun, but the sun had found them. If anyone were to hold the sun, they might hide it away again and keep it for themselves.

Maybe it was better that the sun lay out of reach.

"Cap?" Jungle asked and closed his eyes. "We didn't catch the sun. But do you still think the world is ending?"

Cap's fibers shivered, renewed with energy and certainty. "Nope."

Grimaldia's Lair

Elyse Russell

Grimaldia had a bone to pick.

It was, after all, quite difficult to get the meat out from between her fangs.

She kept it on a leather strap around her neck, and it hung between her six pendulous, shriveled teats. She never bothered to wash it, and dark stains coated the sharpened ivory.

The bone had been taken from one of her victims: an elephant-headed man. After Grimaldia had eaten the man's flesh raw, she pulled a tusk from the skull and set about whittling it to a sharp, utilitarian point.

When she was a young witch, Grimaldia had simply used her own sickle-like talons. Now, though, she was ancient, and her talons were chipped and cracked with age. Where she was once able to shred her victims to death, she now simply used her greater size and strength to quickly snap their necks. This was done more out of exhaustion than mercy. Ideally, she would have liked to play with her victims a bit more.

Hunger pangs gnawed at the witch's belly, forcing her to emerge from her nest. She blinked in the dim light of the great hall, and walked amongst the rows and rows of full-length mirrors. They gleamed dully in the twilight that shone through the cracked glass dome overhead.

For her lair, Grimaldia had chosen an abandoned palace in a distant, ruined city. It was far from any modern civilization, which suited her needs just fine. No angry villagers to deal with, not since most people went to live underground.

The planet had become inhospitable over a period of only a few hundred years, wiping out entire populations, and driving others to seek shelter in subterranean cities. Very few intelligent life forms lingered on the surface. The underground peoples had tunnels that led to enormous enclosed greenhouses.

They only ever felt the sun's rays through the thick layers of glass. Grimaldia wondered what unfiltered rays would do to them. She daydreamed absently about what it would be like to watch one of them die in broad daylight.

Grimaldia, too, rarely felt the sunlight warm her fur. In her case, though, it was simply because the sun heated her to fatal levels very quickly. Hence, she had taken shelter in the palace. After she'd done that, memories of the broader world had faded to mere cobwebs in her mind. She was trapped in this ruin, a sad, sepulchral island in the greater hellscape.

One room, which had once been a library, had been stuffed by the witch from floor to ceiling with the clothing and hair of her victims. There, she would burrow in and curl up each day to rest, her balding tail tucked tightly against her. The paper from the books that once sat on the shelves had been shredded and piled in a corner for a toilet, though old age had made Grimaldia more and more incontinent. She didn't always use the toilet anymore. It was her palace, anyway, and she was completely alone there, after the death of her twin.

The corpse of her sister lay in the dining hall, covered in cobwebs. Occasionally, Grimaldia would go there to converse with her stunted, deformed skull. There were times when she almost wished she hadn't eaten Lionia. Conversation was nice every once in a blue moon, after all. They'd been companions for a few centuries beforehand, until one day, Grimaldia had gotten hungry enough and annoyed enough to just...take a bite. And then keep going, despite her sister's squeals of terror and disbelief.

But she made on well enough without her, though she knew that she was very likely the last of her kind. Though her people had never been very multitudinous, it still pleased her somewhat to know that she was probably the only woman-faced rat left in existence. Certainly, even if there were a few others left, she was the last witch. It gave her a sense of importance and made her feel as though the world belonged to her. Certainly those swarming multitudes breathing and shitting beneath the surface didn't count. They were only meat. Her meat.

In the main hall, she had assembled her hunting mirrors. They were arranged in less-than-orderly rows throughout the room, and there were exactly sixty-six of them. Grimaldia paused to stare at them, her tattered, white ears swiveling and her tail twitching like a dying snake. Her pride and joy, this collection. Each had been taken from a different witch (after she had killed said witch herself). And now, each of them did her bidding alone.

The floor was littered with bones; they crunched beneath Grimaldia's hairy, twisted feet as she made her way to an old, cracked mirror, surrounded by a frame of beautiful gold scrollwork. At least, it was beautiful beneath the heavy layer of dust. It was at least eight hundred years old—nearly as old as Grimaldia herself. As she watched, a fat spider dropped down on a thin strand of web before the mirror's surface. The witch's stomach growled in anticipation as she trailed her gray, lumpy tongue across the reflective surface, leaving behind a sticky coating of saliva. She caught the spider on her tongue and felt it squirm against the roof of her mouth for a moment before she swallowed it whole.

When Grimaldia muttered a few magic words, the saliva she'd left started to move. The surface of the mirror began to bubble and flex beneath the liquid, and Grimaldia's eyes dilated at the sight that slowly came into focus. She leaned closer, her short, human nose twitching above a sparsely-whiskered chin.

Rather than her own reflection, what the witch saw in the mirror was a wolf-headed man walking down a narrow street in some subterranean metropolis. She wondered whether it were somewhere nearby, beneath her very feet perhaps, or if it were leagues away. He had his hands in his pockets, and held his head low and shoulders slumped. When other people passed him, he did not make eye contact.

Grimaldia's tail twitched with excitement. This one looked like just the sort of societal outcast she preferred to catch. Occasionally, she would take someone who would be missed, simply to watch the panic of the rest of the ants, but she could still vaguely remember hunting parties seeking her out. Though the people never breached the surface anymore, she still had an instinctual desire to keep her killings as secretive as possible.

She always watched them for a while, her victims, before snatching them out of their environments. It was one of her few forms of entertainment, and stories added spice to meals. "Knowing where the meat between your teeth has been makes the flavors come alive," her sister used to say. Grimaldia had always agreed. Misery, in particular, was her favorite of seasonings. Even better when the prey was miserable and unhygienic. An unbathed specimen was a delight to her old tastebuds.

And so she watched the wolf-headed man as he turned into a dark alley. She licked her chops as he furtively urinated against a brick building, and then moved on at a shuffle. Smells from the alley drifted up to her nostrils. She could smell his piss. Dank and fetid as this mirror world was, it still seemed like a whiff of fresh air when compared to the familiar stench in the witch's own lair. At least these foul odors were *living* and *juicy*.

Grimaldia watched as her prey finally found his way to one of many poorhouses, where he climbed to the top mattress on a rickety five-level bunk bed. He curled up on his side and started drifting to sleep. Grimaldia bared what yellowed teeth she had left and reached into the mirror. This was perfect.

Harren had had a rough day. Ever since the war between the wolf-heads and the deer-heads, it had been almost impossible to find work. Wolf-heads were painted as unsavory characters—no matter that he was too young to have fought in the skirmishes. He'd heard what people whispered about him and his kind: shifty, untrustworthy, carnivores, backstabbers...the list went on.

Not only could Harren not find work to support himself, but he had also just gotten word that day that his lover had had her memory wiped. She hadn't recognized him when he went to see her. His chest still hurt, and he rubbed at the ache absently as he walked down the dark street.

Perhaps it was a blessing that she no longer remembered him. A blessing, at least, for her. For Harren would never have been able to support a wife. He couldn't very well have asked her to live in the poorhouse with him. She was better off, now, apprenticed to the deer-headed woman who owned an emporium and sold magical truffles.

She would be safe there.

He, it seemed, would never be safe. For just a little while, he hadn't been alone. Now, here he was again, with no family and no lover. And no money or food. He would go to bed hungry again tonight.

With a sigh, Harren ducked into an alley. His bladder was full to bursting, so he stopped to relieve himself where no one could see. He let out a deep sigh as he buttoned the front of his pants back up.

Yes, it really was for the best, he told himself again. *If her master had found out that she was no longer a virgin...*

Harren shuddered. They had taken such risks. He should not have gambled her life, simply because he was so desperate to fill the lonely void. He deserved to feel all of this pain.

No one acknowledged Harren when he entered the poorhouse and climbed straight up the tall ladder to his topmost bunk. The mattress was stuffed with old straw and smelled of mildew and sweat. He didn't own a blanket. Curling up on his side, Harren rested one fuzzy cheek in the palm of his hand and closed his eyes, trying to dispel all thoughts of his former lover and ignore his gnawing, empty belly so that he could get some rest. He'd try to get a job again tomorrow. Somehow.

Just before Harren could drift off to sleep, however, a clawed hand gripped his shoulder. He yelped in surprise, his eyes shooting open. Disbelief made his jaw drop at what he was seeing.

A long, enormous, hairy white arm was reaching out of nowhere. It looked like it was detached and levitating above him. The arm pulled back, taking him with it.

Harren didn't have time to scream before he was yanked into the darkness. On the bunk just below his, an old monkey-headed man grumbled in his sleep and rolled over. No one would ever notice that Harren had disappeared.

Grimaldia heaved the wolf-headed man through the mirror, depositing him on the floor with a *thump*. She cackled and wheezed at his panic-stricken face, pounding heartbeat, and ragged breathing. Sucking air in through her teeth, she savored the scent of his fear. Her nostrils flared with delight and anticipation.

He was a skinny thing, but there was still enough meat on his bones to satisfy her for at least a few days. She would enjoy sucking the marrow from this one. And then she could talk to his skull for a while, too, perhaps. She hadn't added a canid skull to her collection in quite a while.

The woman-faced rat merely watched with amusement as the wolf-headed man tried to scramble away. When he tripped over a giant, fractured bird skull and screamed, she threw her head back and laughed, letting the sound echo through her halls. This was too much fun.

She stalked him. The pair weaved between the mirrors, ducking and dodging. Grimaldia even felt girlish enough to hide momentarily behind one of them before she popped out on the other side with a screech, causing the wolf-head to nearly faint with terror. It was the most entertainment she'd had in ages.

So caught up in the game was she that she didn't notice when her prey found one of the broken mirrors and pocketed a large, jagged shard. None of her other victims had ever fought back (something about being yanked out of nowhere and transported to seemingly another world usually took the spunk right out of them), and so the idea had never occurred to her to, essentially, prey-proof her abode.

When the wolf-headed man suddenly ducked around a mirror and stepped out behind her, she didn't turn quickly enough. Her great bulk and arthritic hips impaired her. He leapt for her, baring his own strong, young fangs, and embedded the shard of mirror right into the back of her neck, where most of her hair-sprouting moles were located.

At first, Grimaldia did not react. She was paralyzed with shock. A chill ran down her spine. She reached up and yanked the shard out, causing blood to spurt forth from her neck. She hardly noticed. Rage was welling up within her, clouding her vision and her judgment. With a mighty swipe of an oversized arm, Grimaldia slashed her talons across the chest of her would-be prey. He cried out and fell back amongst the dust, bones, and debris that littered the floor. Old blood stains, long since browned, looked like a map beneath him. Grimaldia barely remembered maps.

The witch swayed on her feet, the room spinning about her. She saw her grotesque form reflected in each of the mirrors around her.

The crimson blood was soaking down over her dirty white fur. It was so very bright.

The mirrors rattled when Grimaldia's bulk hit the floor with a shuddering *thud*. As the blood began to pool around her and the death rattle escaped her throat, she narrowed her eyes at the last face she would ever see, and she muttered a terrible curse.

Harren stared down at the corpse. He was shaking so hard that his teeth were chattering. His ears were laid back flat against his head, and the deep cuts on his chest bled and ached. Every hair down his back stood on end.

He'd never seen anything like this creature before. She had the body of an enormous rat. Standing, she had been over seven feet tall. But her head…it reminded him somewhat of the monkey-headed people, but there was far less fur on it. She was, in fact, bald. Indeed, even the filth-matted fur on her body was scant, showing the pale, diseased skin underneath. He spied fleas and ticks biting and swelling amongst the folds and wrinkles.

He could only tell that the thing was a female because of the breasts—six of them!—that were now flopped onto the stone floor like deflated wineskins. Each pinkish nipple had sprouted several wiry white hairs. The talons on her hands were four inches long, at least.

And where was he? Harren stood, looking up and blinking for a long moment. It appeared to be a giant hall, with large, stone pillars and several branching corridors. Terrible smells emanated from each of the openings. Everything was covered in a layer of grime, apart from places where the creature had evidently frequently walked, dragging her tail behind her.

That tail twitched once more, sending Harren's heart rate bursting again. When he was sure that it had merely been a death spasm, he continued warily surveying his surroundings.

There was a strange dome of grimy glass above him, shattered in places. Through those holes, he could glimpse far off twinkling lights. They looked like white lights—far different from the yellow gas lamps that he was used to.

The odor of the place was overwhelming. Harren's head began to spin.

I haven't eaten, I've had the fright of my life, and I'm losing blood, Harren thought to himself.

He passed out.

Hours later, Harren awoke, blinking, to the brightest light he'd ever seen. He brought his hands up to shield his eyes, as they stung from the intensity. When his pupils had adjusted somewhat, he stole a quick glance upward.

Instead of darkness with tiny points of white light, he saw a stretch of light blue—the brightest blue he'd ever seen. The intense light that shone on him was coming from an enormous orb up there—one that he couldn't even look at.

Harren got to his feet and began slowly stumbling amongst the mirrors toward a large door, which hung on its hinges. More light was shining through the doorway.

When he stepped through it, Harren gasped with amazement and nearly fainted again. He was in a new world. A bright world. And there was green everywhere.

Colorful purple day-bats swooped overhead, clicking to each other. A pink praying mantis caught a tiny frog and began gnawing on it, perched upon a broad leaf near the door. Vines swung from tall, strange-looking plants, and the ground was carpeted in soft, swishing green strands.

Hesitantly, Harren stepped out of the dark palace into the light, the first of his people to do so in centuries. Perhaps this strange turn of events would work out in his favor, after all.

But the further Harren went into the strange light, the more his skin began to itch. When he reached up to scratch at his ear, clumps of fur came away on his hand. Alarmed, he started to stumble back toward the ruins.

An ear fell off, and then more fur. Harren fell to his knees as his skin disintegrated. As he took his last breath, he heard the echoes of the witch's last hiss.

A ghostly witch's laugh shuddered through his bones before everything dimmed to a familiar black.

The Hunt

Trey Stone

Urok's heavy body slumped against the thick oak, and the wood groaned.

"How much longer?"

Coia turned to look at the shaggy shape. Hot breath clouded the air in front of Urok's face, and her pelt was matted.

"Not far," Coia said. He stopped by a nearby rock and smelled the air. "A day or two, depending on our speed."

"Then it is two," Urok growled. "And it is far. I don't remember it being this far." She heaved for breath, her lumbering body expanding and deflating. The oak creaked and cracked with every movement. "Don't worry your long snout about me," she said when she caught Coia staring. "I just need a moment."

"I don't worry." Coia's ears flared, rising and twisting as the winds moved through the trees.

"Your kind always worry. About the winter. About the forest. About the night and the day." Urok rolled away from the tree, digging deep tracks in the soft ground as she landed on all fours. "Onward, then. I won't be the one who slows this party down."

Coia's ears flicked again and he raised his eyes to the sky. He had almost forgotten about the third member of their *party*, soaring somewhere up there, high above them. It felt both good and unnerving to know that they were not alone. Urok's big, brown shoulder grazed Coia's side as she lumbered past. "You're fast, but you're not that fast. Get up in front."

Coia resorted to four-pawed running, jumping over a small creek and rounding a rock so that he was ahead of Urok, then he stood up on his hind legs and smelled the air again. They were going the right way.

The mountainside became cooler with every step. At first, the trees were sparser, farther apart and fewer between, and now they were all but gone. Coia did not like it. He did not like the wind. He preferred the thick forest of the valley floor, where he knew every twig, log and branch by heart, where he could drop to his fours and dig into the earth, knowing that nobody knew his forest as well as him. When he focused, he could go at almost unhindered speeds. Only the feathered ones could keep up with him there, and only barely.

"When do we eat?" Urok said from behind Coia. The snarl in her voice made it clear that she would have preferred to already be eating, and it sounded like there ought to be a lot of it.

"Soon," Coia said. The winds tore down the mountainside and froze the roots of Coia's gray pelt. Food would do them good. It wouldn't be the warm, rich food they expected, but it would be food and there would preferably be shelter. Urok didn't mind the cold, she probably didn't even notice it through her thick, brown skin, but Coia wasn't built for winter. Frost burned in his nose.

"We should try to get over on the east side before we stop for the night. It'll be warmer there. Less wind."

"I don't care about the wind!" Urok growled. "Food!"

"I know you want to eat, but it will be better if we wait until we're farther along."

Urok growled again, a roar almost, and though Coia couldn't keep from being unsettled by the trembling sound, he knew it was just an empty threat. Urok and her kind had just as much to lose as Coia's. And Coia would outrun her long before Urok managed to clamp down on his neck.

They carried on, following a small gravel path snaking its way to the east. Coia took it without letting Urok know that he was uncertain. It was best to be unwavering.

The sun was far away, hidden away in the depths behind the west side of the mountain and it was almost night when a shadow fell upon them.

"There's a ravine."

Coia hadn't heard neither wings nor talons. In the dark, featherkin were almost invisible, even with Coia's eyesight.

53

"Who goes there?" Urok snarled from the back of the trail.

"Morras," Morras said. He folded his black wings neatly against his side, blending into the backdrop of the night. He leaned on his thin legs, and Coia wondered how those thin, hollow bones could carry such a large body. "There's a ravine. For stopping. For food. Not far, just a little while."

"Thank you, Morras. Will you be joining us tonight?" Coia leered, but tried not to. Morras was never truly with them. He flew, always too high to be easily spotted. He visited occasionally, but always left again quickly. Coia's ears twisted. He suspected Morras wasn't alone.

"Not tonight, not joining." Morras spoke with the unconnected clatter of all beaked creatures. "Crawlers stop, Morras follow."

Coia snarled at the word. Featherkin never said it out loud, but it wasn't a secret that they looked down upon the slow, unimportant creatures that were bound to crawl along the dirt, chained to the earth. In another situation, Coia would have been tempted to jump at the beaked one and tear the wings off his back. Morras never seemed like the fastest, nor the brightest of the lot.

But today, they were allies. Urok had been surprisingly well-behaved so far, barely even snapping at Coia at all—at least not more than Urok's kind usually did. Coia could not be the one who broke the oath.

"Any sign of them?" Coia asked.

Morras' head tilted. "They're here. They've seen us coming. They follow on the mountainside. You'll see." With that, he spread his wings and leaped forward. Coia instinctively bared his teeth and raised his hackles, ready to drop to all paws, but Morras disappeared into the black night.

"What did he mean?" Urok asked as she lumbered closer.

"No idea. Let's carry on to the ravine. Your talk of food has made me hungry."

The ravine was barely a crack in the mountainside. For Urok, it was nothing but a nuisance, and there was no way she could fit her shaggy pelt between the narrow rocks. She snarled and growled, eventually circling herself before plodding down against the side of a rock in the middle of the path.

"Food!" Her roar trembled on the wind.

They had brought food. They knew they couldn't very well forage

54

while they traveled into mountain territory, and while they didn't dare bring fish, they couldn't be starving.

"Empty your baskets."

Urok had carried the food in two woven containers carried across her wide back. They were almost empty now, and Urok threw her back so that the remaining contents spilled on the ground between them.

Yams and beets. From the small, wet fields where Coia's forests crossed over onto the plains. Urok's wide muzzle grinned and she didn't cast a second glance at Coia before she started devouring them whole.

Coia jumped nimbly over the mountain path, grabbed one of the larger yams, and bounded back to the ravine. With the food on the ground between his forepaws, he lay down on his front and ate with his teeth, like before. Like Urok did.

The sound of Urok's eager chewing resonated in front of him, and Coia allowed himself to rest his eyes momentarily. Soon they would have to carry on.

The moon had passed half the sky when Coia woke abruptly. His ears twisted, eyes quick to adjust to the night. At first he thought it might have been Urok, but the giant was fast asleep, snoring and rumbling like an avalanche.

Coia's hackles rose. A sound, at the edge of their small camp. Something clattered on the ground. Morras? Coia drew a breath through his nose, searching for a scent he could know. Whatever it was, it wasn't featherkin. It wasn't Morras.

"Who's there?"

No time for games. Coia was used to being the sneak in the shadows, but whoever was out there had the upper hand. Perhaps calling them out could scare them into thinking they weren't as secretive as they thought.

Coia rose to four paws. He didn't like being chained to the ground, not like Urok who didn't seem to carry any pride under her thick pelt, but Coia couldn't deny that he was faster and more dangerous like this. "Who's there?" He growled now, stepping out of the ravine.

Behind them, the path they had come from snaked around the mountainside. In front of them was the same. Above and below them, the rock was too steep for Coia and Urok to climb, at least in the middle of the night, without risk of falling to their deaths.

If it came to fighting, the camp would give them most room to defend themselves.

"Urok, wake up!" Coia leaped over to his companion, rising onto hind paws as he neared and sending a soft kick into the brown fur. "There's someone here."

"Kick me again, *howler*, and I'll tear your head off by the tips of your ears and throw you down the mountain." Urok's voice was cold and harsh. "I heard them too. Do you sense them?"

"No. It's too dark and there's too many rocks to hide behind. They're not featherkin, I know that much. It's not Morras."

"Then it is *them*," Urok said, rising onto fours. "And we know we have come to the right place." Urok continued rising, and Coia had to step back as the giant grew larger. Even standing, Coia barely reached Urok's shoulders. Now that Urok rose to her hinds, she was enormous. Her kind had always preferred to travel on fours. Coia assumed it had to do with their cumbersome size; it was easier to maneuver and remain balanced low to the earth, everyone knew that. But when they wanted to make an impression they could rise just as well as any others.

"We are just two!" Even the wind could not tear away Urok's thick voice. "A third sometimes joins us from the sky. We come only to hold council—you'll know we speak the truth, because we ourselves are not known allies." Urok's wide paw dangled next to Coia's head. The claws weren't as sharp as his, but they were thicker and longer. The paw nudged him. "Tell them," Urok grumbled.

"The old one speaks the truth!" Coia felt he had to howl to be heard over the wind. "We come with words, nothing else. Ask our feathered friend if you don't believe us, he'll tell you the same thing—if you can find him."

They stood there, paw by paw, and stared into the night. Urok sniffed against the wind. "Are they still there?"

Coia wasn't sure. "Yes, they're there. Somewhere, in the dark." It tasted like a lie, but it felt better than admitting to Urok that whoever was there managed to avoid both of them.

"Surely, you know why we've come!" Coia yelled louder now, and he saw Urok's thick neck turn to look down on him from the corner of his eye. "You must have seen it yourselves. It spreads like wildfire through the lowlands. It is not safe anymore. It can't be any different up here."

Then, another clattering noise, like the one that had woken Coia. Two white shapes flew through the darkness, straight toward them. Coia stepped back, ready to drop to fours, but Urok remained standing, vigilant and unmoving. The shapes landed not far in front of them, smacking against the ground.

"Are those bones?" Coia frowned at the two things, and couldn't help baring teeth. It looked like many small pointed bones bound together on a thick string.

Urok fell forward, landing with a groan on her fore paws on the gravel path. "Not bones," she said, approaching the things and turning one over with her claws. Coia saw now that one was larger than the other. "Antlers."

Coia approached alongside Urok, but kept his distance. "You've seen these before?"

Urok leaned back, falling onto her rump and sitting. She grabbed one of the things. "Put them on, *howler*." A sigh escaped the brown giant. "It's an invitation."

Coia grabbed the smaller one, holding it out in front of him with an outstretched limb. "A necklace?"

"Almost," Urok said with a strained voice, and Coia turned to look in horror at Urok's pained face. "It's a muzzle."

The string of antlers was tight around her head and the many white points bit into Urok's fur. She had put hers on without trouble, alone, as if this was a thing she had worn dozens of times.

"We're near now," Urok rumbled through clamped jaws. "They'll be expecting us."

For once, Urok led the way. They carried on up the mountain path, lit by the dull moonlight. A narrow line of beaten gravel twisted along the hillside, and Coia knew that they were going the right way just as Urok knew—by the scent.

It was thick and bitter on the wind. Hooves and fur, and antlers and horns; Coia didn't understand how he hadn't smelled it earlier.

He drew a deep breath, trying not to make the muzzle bite harder into his jaw than it already was, when he walked straight into Urok's backside. The antlers stabbed at the soft black skin of his nose and Coia winced.

"Why did we stop?" It was hard to speak through the mask. Every movement threatened to tear holes in fur and skin, and when they dug deep, they never came back out.

"We're here." Urok threw her head forward.

Coia leaned out to see, walking slowly around the massive body. There was an open space in front of them, a clearing of sorts, made of rock and gravel. The sand looked to be beaten down to a fine, even powder. First it confused Coia what could have done such a thing, then he saw all the small circles in the gray ground and recognized the hoof prints. Behind them, the thin path crawled back to where they had rested, and in front of them, between two tall and jagged boulders, a similar path carried on forward. There was nothing else, no other places to go that didn't require scaling a steep, slick rock first.

They stood in a pit.

They had walked into a trap.

One of *them* stood upon a tall rock at the other end of the pit. Matted sour-gray hair lay in long clumps down his thick chest and arms, and the hair on his cheeks and chin was pointed and colored with reds and blacks. Thick, curved horns adorned his head, bending backward and revealing many scars and chips along their front. Powerful hoofed feet kept him perfectly balanced upon the thin sliver of rock that he stood upon.

"Why have you come?" he bleated.

"We come with grave news—" Coia began, but a trembling bleat stopped him.

"Let the old one speak!"

Coia saw that there were more of them now, crawling onto the rocks from every direction. Browns, grays, whites, some with curved horns and some with many-pronged antlers. Some were short and stacked, while others stood tall and elegant. Coia had never seen such an ensemble of creatures.

"Speaking is difficult, with your gift," Urok said. It came out with a growl that Coia suspected was unintentional.

"That is the sole purpose of it," a soft voice from somewhere to the side of them said. "Try, or leave." It was a young antlered beast with light brown fur and dark eyes.

Urok bowed her head. "We come to talk of the plague. It has swallowed much of the forest, the plains and the lowlands. We don't know how far it reaches, where it comes from, or how to cure it, all we know is that it spreads. Our dark friend, Morras, is somewhere up above us.

He came to discuss the same thing as us—"

"We have already spoken to Morras, and sent him on his way." The curved horned one spoke again, and his voice was steadier now. It echoed inside the pit, bouncing between the rocks and ringing in Coia's ears.

"So you know of what we speak?" Urok sounded almost surprised. "Are you afflicted too? Your kind also succumbs to the madness?"

For a moment no one replied. Coia began to wonder if maybe they struggled to hear what Urok was saying through the sharp muzzle. Then the horned one reacted.

He *jumped* down into the pit. Those at the edge of the circle drew sharp breaths, and Coia thought he heard one of them yell. He wasn't sure because he was too focused on the creature. His thick neck and muscled arms were even bigger close up. Sure, Urok would not have struggled to maul the creature to death, but had Coia been alone, even without the muzzle, he wouldn't have stood a chance.

A glint of something in the horned one's eyes reminded Coia of the myths from before, and when the creature stepped closer and the light of the moon caught that black oblong pupil, dancing in that yellow liquid, Coia recoiled.

Ram.

Coia had heard of them, but never seen one. He hadn't dared think they were real. They were ancient, older even than Urok's kind. Some said they communed with the depths of the earth, that flames burned were their hooves trod, and that their bleats could shatter bone. Even before the world changed, they walked around on twos.

"Of course, we know of what you speak, old one. It has been known for generations. I have seen minds shrivel, I have seen the afflicted forced onto front hooves, and their speech stolen from them." The ram stepped closer, narrowing his evil eyes. Urok's breath visibly moved the gray hair on the ram's chest. "What do *you* propose we do about it?"

"We propose a bargain. Winters are getting longer, harvests shorter. The valley runs wet every summer, rivers overflow and the crops die. I'm sure the mountains aren't faring any better?" The ram's eyes narrowed and Urok sighed. "Or do your kind blossom up here, among rock and dust? It's colder than I remember." Urok shivered, and made an effort to move her heavy head around the pit, looking at those that had gathered. Only now did Coia notice how ragged, thin and measly they all looked. Not one was muscled and strong like the ram, and most seemed to freeze just as much as Coia did against the wind.

"All kinds struggle in harsh times. That's what makes them harsh. What is your point?" The ram drew long breaths between bleats, buffing his chest against Urok's snout.

"We need to eat. All of us. Those that have succumbed to the plague are lost. Let us revisit the pacts we forged centuries ago. Let us hunt again."

"They mean to eat us!" Screams arose around the pit, and echoed between the antlered ones in a cacophonous panic. Coia smelled the fear spreading through the throng of creatures and saw antlered spears rise high above their shoulders. He took an uneasy step back, stopping against Urok's rough fur.

"Silence!" the ram shouted. His voice was harsh when raised. "Is that your truth? You want to...You ask to eat those that succumb to the wilderness?"

"We ask to hunt again. Let us hunt the afflicted that wander out of our cities, beyond our borders. We can feed a whole generation that way, and never have to touch a harvest again."

"Why would we allow that? Those are still our family. It's our friends that roam out there."

"Once perhaps, but not anymore. We've seen it ourselves, in the lowlands. There's no recognition in the eyes of those that are lost. They are wild, feral creatures. My own kin attacked me and mine when we tried to commune with them." Urok drew a breath. "We had to slay him. And, as is the natural order of things, we left him for the scavengers."

"It is true," Morras cawed. "The old one speaks true." He sat perched high above the pit of rocks, his head flicking this way and that in the dark night.

"In return, we would give you our harvest. Return to the lowlands. Feed upon the grass and the leaves, the flowers and the fruits. We would turn the earth for you. Work the land. We would give them all up for the hunt."

The ram and Urok stared at one another before the ram turned to Coia. "What do you say, young gray-pelt? Will your kind take part in this deal?"

Coia was glad for the muzzle then, because he could hide much of his uncertainty behind the antlers that clamped around his jaw. "I... No." He swallowed. "We were asked to come here because we each knew one part of the truth. Urok and Morras know the reality we are facing, first hand, as they've spoken it. There's an order to things, a pattern in nature that we could follow where—yes, some would suffer—but others would prosper. There's still fish in the rivers and roots in the ground. It wouldn't have to be a slaughter."

"Speak plainly, *howler*!" the ram bleated. "Why are you here?"

"To tell you that some of my kin have chosen the route we speak of already. A pack, larger than any you have ever seen, has already left the plains. Instead of mourning their kin and shielding themselves from the plague, they have joined forces. Dropped to fours, willingly, and adapted to the wilderness. They held no council, respected no pact, and they are already hunting. They won't settle for just the afflicted. They'll come for you, whether you agree to our proposition or not."

The moon twinkled in the ram's oblong eyes. He turned to Urok. "And if we refuse your offer? If we deny you your hunt, old one, what then?"

Urok sighed heavily before sitting back on her rump. Coia glanced at her, thinking she was tired of arguing, of talking so much. Urok rarely spoke, and when she did her words were usually few.

"Then," she said, after a long moment's contemplation. She began growling, baring her teeth, and her back arched as she rose to her hind legs. With a sharp crack, the muzzle snapped and Urok roared. "I fear that my kin will come for you regardless. And who will protect you against the howlers then, Gorne? When we all descend into the madness of the past. The hunt is coming, whether you like it or not. Too many have already suffered. Let's stand side by side, this time. Hoof and paw."

Gorne looked up at Urok, craning his neck. His horns lay curved against his shoulders. "As allies then," he said, casting a glance at Coia. "Old, and new."

The People of the Roots

Varya Kartishai

Baru was hungry, but the basket that he kept his gold-wing beetles in was nearly empty. Org seeds lay outside in drifts against the roots of his tree. They could be eaten, but they had a slight bitterness and the husks were useless, fit only to be tossed into the breeze. He shrugged and walked through the low tunnel to the entrance to fill his belt pouch. On the way back he smiled into each of the shining gold beetle cases hanging on the painstakingly smoothed walls. He knew the reflected faces that returned his smile were his own, but the varying contour of each gave back a slightly different face. He liked to pretend that they were his brothers.

He had almost completed the burrow when Elda, his mother, left him to pursue her own concerns. She had warned him that the time would come when he would have to go. Sometimes he wondered whether she had found another mate and he had real brothers some-where. He liked to imagine that his mother had told his father where to find him and one day he would arrive at the burrow, full of tales about his adventures. Or that perhaps she might be waiting for him to come find her.

As time passed it had become more difficult to remember her face. The only memories that remained clear were the soft green of her fur, so different from the deep blue of his own, and her gentle voice, telling him the things he would need to know when he reached his full growth and she was no longer there. If he had known how empty the burrow would feel without her, he might have begged her to stay, but she had seemed so sure that he was old enough to manage on his own. The only tangible thing she had left him was the little flute he had hung beside the beetle cases. She had helped him fashion it, then taught him to play the special call that might bring him a mate, if there was a female near.

Even now, as he prepared to leave his comfortable burrow to find another place where gold-wing beetles were plentiful, he couldn't imagine another female taking his mother's place.

He finished his unsatisfying meal, trying not to think of how much work went into digging a proper tunnel, then went back outside to cut a slab of bark to transport his few possessions. The piece of smooth stone he had sharpened into a cutting tool peeled the bark neatly and he was able to cut only as much as he needed. He apologized to the tree for the discomfort he had caused it, cut neat slits at the front corners, and knotted rope he had twisted from dry grass into them to make a handle.

He decided to get a comfortable night's sleep and leave in the morning, but sleep eluded him and the sun rose before he was ready. He took a last look at his beautiful cases, then wrapped them in the winter blanket he had woven from root fibers and seed fluff. Finally he ate the last of his gold-wing beetles, loaded the cases on the sled, then whispered farewell to his burrow and the kindly tree that had sheltered him for so long.

He had never traveled farther from his burrow than the little stream that flowed nearby for water, next to the stand of sa bushes where he collected beetles for his larder. Now, unsure where he would find another stream, he filled the water containers that he had woven and sealed with fire-hardened clay and added them to the sled. Last, he carefully tied down his clay fire box filled with live coals and set off. The trees in this part of the wood stood far enough apart to make walking easy, with bushes and grass for cover. There were too many dangers to venture into the open—hunting birds could carry him off, and there were animals larger than himself who would think him as edible as the beetles he hunted. His mother had trained him to recognize the strong scent they used to mark their territory, and he was prepared to hide if he detected it.

The thought of unlimited space stretching around him made him feel dizzy. He had to speak sternly to himself before he was able to go on. He'd managed to travel some distance, but there had been no sign of gold-wing beetles, or the damp areas they were found in. He began to wonder if anything else in the area might be edible and plucked an experimental pawful of a seed-bearing grass that seemed plentiful. The dry seeds had a pleasant taste with none of the bitterness of the org seeds, and he decided to empty those out and refill his pouch, then stop to take a quick meal with a little water.

He was uneasy about settling in an area without water nearby, and there had been no sign yet of another stream. He looked carefully around for danger, finally pulling his sled under a thick cluster of fana bushes, then sat down with his back against a tree that reminded him of his old friend. Small birds twittered musically above him as he ate, but when he reached into his sled and pulled out the little flute to try to copy their song it had exactly the opposite effect. They began to twitter more noisily and hop up and down on the branches, as though he had said something rude. He sighed and was about to put the flute away when he caught a familiar scent. Ruta flowers, like those his mother had liked to twine around her neck.

Impulsively, he began to play the call for a mate she had taught him. He heard rustling in the bushes a little distance away but there was no one visible, so he continued playing, adding little ornaments to the tune as he watched the spot where he thought the noise had come from. He thought he saw movement behind the leaves.

A small green figure slipped out of the bushes and stood shyly watching him. As he kept playing, it cautiously moved closer. Suddenly there was an almost silent rustle of wings; air rushed past his head as one of the predator birds swooped toward the figure. He dropped his flute and, almost without thought, picked up a large stick and leaped at the bird, managing to catch a pawful of its underfeathers as it snatched up the stranger. Holding tightly to the feathers with one paw, he reached up with the other, hammering at the cruel beak with the stick. The bird, far larger than he, was thrown off balance by the unexpected attack. It squawked an indignant protest, opening its beak and dropping its prize, which scuttled rapidly into the bushes. Baru quickly let go and dived in after it. The stranger clung to him, trembling, as the bird screamed and paced back and forth outside their refuge. Finally it flew away, muttering disgustedly, and Baru recovered enough to ask, "Are you hurt?"

"You saved my life. How could you be so brave?"

"It was my fault. If I had not distracted you, you would have seen the bird yourself."

"My name is Auran."

"I am Baru."

"I have never seen you before. Do you live nearby?"

"Not too far from here. I was searching for a place for a new burrow. The gold-wing beetles are gone from my old one."

"Do you like them? They are my favorite food."

"Very much. I stayed as long as I could, but there are no more. On the way here, I found some grass seeds that were not bad. Would you like to try them?" He opened his pouch to show her.

"My mother called those zobar seeds. Thank you, but I already have a store in my burrow. It is not far, would you like to stop and rest a while?"

"How kind, I have been traveling since early morning, and I am tired and hungry. Would your mate mind if I intruded?"

She smiled shyly. "I have no mate. I have never felt the need for one."

"Are you never lonely?"

"Sometimes, but no mate is better than living with someone who is not pleasant to be with."

She turned away and slipped into a crevice under a tree root. Baru retrieved his flute, took the rope of his sled and followed her. Outside, the opening was barely wide enough for his sled, but inside it grew larger. He stared admiringly at the burrow, very much like his own, except that there were no beetle cases on the smooth walls. "Did you dig all this yourself?'

"My mother showed me how. After she left I was able to finish it."

"You look too delicate to have done so much work. Did it take very long?"

"It took me some time to get it right. What are all those bundles on your sled?"

"Just some necessities; a winter blanket, extra food and water and my collection of gold-wing beetle cases. They looked so nice on my walls, I could not bear to leave them behind."

"I never thought of hanging them up. How do you make them stay in place?"

"They are very light, a thorn driven into the wall will hold them."

Neither could think of anything else to say, and there was silence for a while until Auran asked, "Can I offer you some refreshment?"

"Thank you, but I have supplies, and there is no need to use yours."

They stopped talking again and sat uneasily, not looking at each other until Auran asked in a low voice, "Were you never lonely after your mother left?"

Baru answered, "Often, but afterwards I began to hang the beetle cases on the walls. I pretended the reflections of my own face were my brothers who were visiting me."

"I understand why you took them with you. Tell me, was that a mating call you were playing before we met?'

"I think so. My mother taught it to me, but I never tried it before. I was surprised and pleased when you answered."

"I felt compelled to respond, but I was not pleased. The compulsion shocked me. I should warn you, I am not sure that I want a mate. The idea of producing a child who will never know its father is disturbing, and I could not bear the thought of leaving it all alone and going off to find a new mate. Did you know your own father?"

"No, but is that not how our people always behave?"

"Yes. But what would happen if we behaved differently?"

"I never thought of such a thing."

"Baru, you seem likable and I am as lonely as you. Would you like to stay here for a while, as friends, and see whether we enjoy each other's company?"

"As friends, not mates? Perhaps, if you have enough room for us both, we could try. There is no one here to judge us."

"I have just finished digging a storage room. The walls aren't smoothed, but if you wouldn't mind that, you could move in there with your belongings."

She pointed to a roughly hollowed out space on one side. Baru drew his sled into it and unpacked his belongings, propping up his beetle cases against the walls as Auran watched. "Would you like to hang those toward the front of the tunnel where they would catch the light? I think I would enjoy looking at them."

"Gladly."

They both liked the idea of companionship. Baru pulled fresh grass and made himself a comfortable bed, then spread his blanket over it. Auran exclaimed at it. "Where did you get such a lovely, warm thing?"

Baru explained with modest pride that he had made it, and she asked, "Could you teach me how it is done?"

He felt pleasure that she appreciated his handiwork, and showed her how he had woven twisted root fibers into a netting, offering to help her start a blanket of her own and show her the best kinds of seed fluff to use for warmth. She vowed to make one before the cold weather arrived. "I covered myself with dry grass last winter, but this would be so much better."

He moved the empty sled into a corner and hung his twig flute on the wall. The beetle cases could wait until morning.

Auran reached up and ran her paw with its sensitive fingers across the flute. "Your mother taught you to play this. Do you think I could learn?"

"There aren't many notes. If you practice every day, you soon learn. I will show you how to make one, so you can use it whenever you want to."

"Would you like something to eat? I generally have some root broth before I go to sleep. There is some ready and it won't take long to heat up."

Baru remembered his mother preparing hot broth in the evening. He had always regretted that she hadn't taught him to cook. He agreed enthusiastically and Auran moved to a little niche in the wall, brushed the ashes from a small bed of coals and blew on them. When a tiny flame appeared she added wisps of dried grass and twigs and placed a clay-covered basket over it. Soon there was a delicious smell. She divided the basket's contents between two small bowls, handed one to Baru and warned him not to burn his tongue.

"Thank you. I had forgotten how much I liked my mother's broth."

Auran finished her broth quickly, and they sat together for a while. Eventually, she yawned.

"I am ready to sleep now. is there anything you need?"

"No. I cannot thank you enough for your hospitality."

"Then I will settle for the night." She hesitated a moment. "It is nice to have someone to talk to."

Next morning Baru awoke, disoriented at first until he remembered where he was. Auran was gone, but after he had tidied his sleeping place he heard soft footsteps, and she entered with a container of water and a small basket. He took her burdens from her.

"Is there water near here? I didn't see any on my way."

"There is a small spring not far away, hidden behind some large rocks. Also, I found a few gold-wing beetles. We can share them."

"Thank you. What can I do in return?"

"It is hard to explain, but I think we both need companionship. Just talk a little about how you spent your days before you left your burrow, and after we have eaten, perhaps you can show me how to make a flute so I can begin learning to play. We can put off making fixed plans until we know each other better."

After they ate, Baru carefully set aside his empty beetle cases to dry. Auran watched and copied his actions with her own cases, then he led her outside to find suitable fallen twigs, still moist enough to be shaped into a flute. When they had enough he showed her how to hollow the pith, leaving a little at the very end for a plug, and cut them into graduated lengths, with the thickest ones cut longest. Finally he showed her how to shape flattened pieces for top and bottom supports and bind all together in order of size with twisted grass rope. When it was finished, she blew softly into the largest twig and was delighted to produce a tiny note. Baru praised her. "Good! When you have practiced, you will be able to make a louder sound."

Auran thanked him, and suggested that, as the sun had gotten high while they worked, they might like to have a bowl of broth. This time she had thickened it with ground grass seeds, making it more filling than the meal they had eaten the night before. While they ate, she remarked that Baru had so many skills that she lacked, that she hoped he would stay long enough to teach her as many as he had patience for.

He had never thought of his skills as being something to admire, and felt warmth toward her for seeing value in the things he could do. Taking out his own flute, he showed her how to form the loud and soft notes and how to combine them to make tunes. She learned quickly and they spent the afternoon playing tunes at the entrance to the burrow until the light began to fade. Auran led the way back inside, suggesting that Baru might like to hang up his beetle cases while she took care of their dinner. Then she turned toward the fire niche and mixed something in her cooking pot. Baru realized that he had enjoyed Auran's company so much, he'd forgotten his treasured cases. He spent a few minutes hanging them in what seemed to him to be a pleasing arrangement, then leaned against the opposite wall to admire them, savoring the pleasant smells coming from the fire. It had been a long time since he could remember feeling so content.

Days passed, one after another, and neither of them could imagine how they had endured being alone for so long. By the time fall approached, Auran had become fairly proficient on her flute and had gotten into the habit of practicing daily at the entrance of the burrow. One morning she felt that she was being watched and realized there was a male stranger standing only a few yards away, smiling at her,.

"I was enjoying your music. What is your name, lovely female?"

"Auran." She frowned. "I was not playing a mating call."

"I would not expect that from a female, but the music drew me. My name is Sani."

The sound of Sani's voice drew Baru to the entrance. At the sight of Auran speaking with a strange male, he felt a surge of annoyance and broke into their conversation. "Who are you?"

"Forgive my intrusion, are you this lady's mate?"

"We have not yet finalized any arrangements."

"Then I hope you will not find my presence unwelcome."

"That depends on what you are seeking here."

"I admit I am looking for a mate, but it was the music that drew me. If the lady is not interested in me as a mate, perhaps you would permit me to settle nearby. I am lonely, and I would like companionship."

"If you would move out of earshot, we can discuss the possibility."

Sani nodded, and moved back into the trees while the other two withdrew into the burrow. Baru began, "I find myself uneasy at the presence of another male, but the burrow and the decision are yours."

"Baru, I have enjoyed the time we have spent together very much. If you would like to have me as a mate, I am willing to consider it, but only if you would consider making a longer arrangement than is customary."

"I would like nothing better. But how does that solve our problem with Sani?"

"If he is truly seeking only companionship, we should have no problem with his finding a mate and digging his own burrow in the area."

Baru decided Auran was right. Sani was still waiting outside. When Baru told him what Auran had suggested, he replied that he would be willing to go on seeking for a mate of his own if he could share their company. Baru went back in, and was delighted to see that Auran was wearing a wreath of flowers around her neck.

"I don't know whether there is a ceremony for mating, but I thought flowers would be nice."

"Auran, you are more beautiful to me than the flowers. I am very happy to be your mate as long as you will allow me to stay with you."

They looked into each other's eyes, and embraced for the first time. Auran suggested that the small storage chamber would be warmer for sleeping, and they could keep the larger main chamber for their mutual belongings. They spent that night together in comfort, happier than either had ever been.

When they went outside next morning, Sani was waiting near the entrance with a strange female. He introduced her as Roda, then asked their opinion on a location for their new burrow. Auran suggested a site on the other side of the spring, close to the water—near enough for companionship, but far enough away for privacy. The couple agreed, and Sani led Roda away to search for an appropriate tree. Baru and Auran spent some time gathering seeds and roots to replace their dwindling supplies, then Auran took her flute from the wall and sat by the burrow entrance to practice, where Baru joined her. They played together for a time before they noticed they had an audience. Sani and Roda, earth-stained from their labor on the new burrow, were seated a short distance away, listening intently. When Sani saw that Baru was aware of him, he got up and came closer. He praised the music, then asked where they had learned so many tunes. Baru smiled and told him they came to him from listening to the birds' songs and the sounds of water, and anyone who wished could copy them.

Roda, who had been listening silently, asked if they would like to share some roots she had roasted over a fire—like Auran, she too had cooking skills. Baru wondered if only females were trained in cooking. They were roots he had eaten before, but only boiled, and the difference in taste amazed him. After downing his portion, he said it was a shame that skills such as this could not be shared and preserved for the use of all, rather than being lost when a parent moved off and left a nearly grown child to fend for itself. They'd all had the same thought at one time or another.

They spoke about it and, after much argument, agreed to remain together as a group for more than the single season that was customary for a mated pair. Sani was concerned that if too many of them collected in one vicinity they would be a more tempting target for the predator beasts, who could smell them and would not be deterred by underbrush. Baru agreed that it could become dangerous, but four of them were too few to draw much attention, and they would have time to arrange a system of defense before young ones arrived. Sani suggested that, once he and Roda had finished their burrow, they might all work together to make an enclosure out of piled stones, high enough to slow an attack by predators. Baru offered to begin work at once, with the others joining in when they had leisure. He suggested that instead of merely running away or hiding, they could pile heaps of small stones at safe locations which could be thrown at the predators if they attempted to enter the living area. Auran thought that if they dug a tunnel to the spring they could travel safely underground to get water. Baru realized that he was beginning to feel less like prey and more in control of his own security. Roda suggested the possibility of uprooting thorn bushes to plant inside the stone barricade, and tying the branches overhead to serve as a shelter from attack by hunting birds. The thought of moving plants from one place to another for their own convenience was new, and they decided to try with a few small and easily manageable plants to see if it could be done.

It had grown late, and they all had much to think about. Baru found this sharing of thoughts with contemporaries gave him a feeling of companionship very different from the patient instruction his mother had given him. He realized he would miss it when the group broke up in the future, as they had planned, and wondered how to prolong their relationship. When they separated for the night and returned to their own burrows, Auran prepared the thickened broth with roots that Baru had liked so much, and while they were eating, she asked, "Have you noticed that the others have never heard the tunes you play on your flute? Do you know that it is different from the flutes others use?"

Baru had no idea what she was talking about. "Different how?"

She replied, "Yours has twelve pipes bound together, so that more complex tunes are possible. Most of the flutes I have seen when males came looking for a mate used only one or two pipes, some had holes bored into them so that the notes could be changed by covering the holes, but none of them could produce as many notes as yours."

"The only other flute I have seen is the one my mother had, and I copied it to make my own. I never thought to ask her where she got it. Perhaps it was a gift from my father. Have you seen many other flutes?"

"There were some other males who came to play for me, but their music did not attract me. I hid until they gave up and went away."

"I am glad you waited for me."

"So am I." She offered a small, almost shy smile. "I was drawn to your flute music, and your bravery in rescuing me from the predator bird won my heart from the beginning."

"You never told me that before."

"No, but I thought this would be a good time. If the signs my mother told me to look for are correct, you will become a father soon, and unless you have changed your mind, I am glad we will be staying together to raise our child."

Baru was stunned, then overjoyed at the thought of being the father of a family. He held Auran close, and told her how happy he was at the thought of being with her and the child to come. He had no idea what would be expected of him, and asked Auran if there was anything she would need.

"My mother told me only a little of what to expect myself. She said my instincts would take over when the time came, but I don't mind telling you I am a little nervous about the process. It should be about six seven-days before it arrives, and it is very reassuring to think that I will not be alone. It is such a comfort to have you here. I have been wondering whether a child of yours might inherit your musical skills. I think they might be unusual among our people. Perhaps your father had them."

That had not occurred to Baru, and he wondered what his father had been like. He had enjoyed sharing his music with the others in their little group, but none of them except Auran had copied his flute and none of them seemed able to coax as much out of their instruments as he did. Auran practiced diligently every day, but only tried to reproduce the tunes he played, and had never produced tunes of her own. Sani's flute was closest to the design of Baru's, although it had only five pipes. He had spent some time learning how to use it for tunes other than the mating call, but he too played only Baru's tunes, and had been heard to complain that the music was too complex for him to master. Baru shared his thoughts with Auran. She replied, "I have been thinking more and more about how you differ from Sani and probably other males. I like the differences very much and hope that they will be passed on to our child."

Baru found the thought of having a child who might be like him very pleasant. He asked Auran again if there was anything he could do to help her get ready for the child, and after a little thought she said, "You have so many useful skills, perhaps you might like to prepare a bed and a small blanket for it, and an extra bowl for it to use when it becomes large enough to take solid food."

Baru had never felt so appreciated, he could not understand how other males left their mates so easily. For his own part, he felt he would stay as long as Auran would allow his presence.

That evening, after they had eaten, they went to the entrance of the burrow to play their flutes, and were joined by Sani and Roda. The music they were producing seemed better than ever, and Baru had almost lost himself in the joy of being part of it when Auran nudged him and whispered in his ear. "There seems to be someone in the bushes over there. If you watch, you will see the branches are moving slightly, and there is no wind."

He looked in the direction she was pointing, and thought he saw a shape behind the leaves. "It is too small to be a predator. If we ignore it, perhaps it will come out into the open." They continued playing, and finally a little green figure emerged. There was something familiar about it, and Baru suddenly realized it reminded him of Elda, his mother, but this figure moved slowly, not gracefully and rapidly as his mother had, and there were streaks of gray in its fur. As it approached, Baru got a clearer view of its face and memories overwhelmed him. It could be no one else!

Had she been ill? What had happened to change her so? Laying down his flute, he ran toward her. "Mother, I have missed you!"

She did not answer at once, but threw herself into his arms and wept. When she recovered herself she said brokenly, "My dear son, I was afraid I had changed too much for you to recognize me."

"Have you been ill?"

"This change comes to all of us, it is part of growing older. I am sorry not to have returned sooner, but so glad I was able to find you at last. Who are these people you are making music with?"

"This is Auran, my mate, soon to be the mother of my child, and these are my friends and neighbors, Sani and Roda."

"She is lovely. I am glad to know you have found such a fine mate. I have been trying to find your father. He had a real gift for music; when I heard you playing I thought it might be him."

"Do you know where he went when he left you?"

She shook her head. Auran broke in, asking, "Now that you have come, would you like to stay with us? I would welcome your help when the child comes."

"If you would like to have me. It is not so easy to have a child alone."

Auran smiled. "Baru will be here also. We have agreed to remain together longer than is usual, but he knows nothing about having a child."

"Of course not, males have never taken part in raising children."

"We are planning to change some of that. Come inside and share our evening meal." She took Elda's arm and led her into the burrow.

Meanwhile Sani and Roda had stopped playing and were preparing to return to their own place. Roda asked Baru if he would mind her asking his mother some questions about having children, as she suspected she might also be with child. He promised to let her talk to his mother when she had gotten settled. When he entered the burrow he found Elda and Auran deep in conversation.

"Baru, did you know that your mother has never taken another mate, but has been searching for your father since she left you?"

"I had no idea. Was he as special as that?"

"I thought so," Elda replied. "I was shattered when he left, although you were a great consolation. I am sorry to tell you, you have no brothers or sisters, but I am looking forward to seeing the new little one when it arrives. It appears that you have inherited many of your father's traits, and I hope your child will have them also. Our people have been stagnating for generations, but he was different. You have his musical talents and Auran tells me you are clever with your hands. It seems you are also prepared to change the way our people live."

Auran interrupted by handing them both bowls of thickened broth and cakes made from toasted and pounded seeds.

"I see you have cooking skills as well as musical talents," Elda said with a kindly smile. "My son has made an excellent choice in a mate."

Auran was pleased—she had been feeling the lack of her own mother very much and wanted to get along well with Elda.

After they finished eating, Baru went outside and collected fresh grasses for his mother's bed. There was plenty of space for it in the larger chamber. He suggested that Elda might like to rest since it was still so soon after her travels, and she agreed, thanking them both for their hospitality. They retired to the inner room, and soon all were asleep, tired from the emotional strain of the reunion.

When they awoke, Baru and Auran heard movement in the next room and smelled something delicious. Elda had already prepared toasted seedcakes for their breakfast. Auran hugged her, and said again how glad she was that Elda had joined them. She took Elda outside to show her the spring, and on the way back they met Roda, who was on her way to the burrow to see if Elda had rested enough to be ready to talk to her.

"It is so good to be welcomed. I have been very lonely in my search for Baru's father."

"Do you think he may have met with an accident?"

"I have no way of knowing that. The way we live makes it impossible to keep track of each other. Even if we become fond of one another, we end by separating and living alone."

Roda replied, "I never thought of things being different, but now I can think of nothing else than getting to know my own child and letting it know Auran's child, so that neither one ever has the horrible loneliness I grew up with."

Auran asked, "Do you know when our people began leading such solitary lives?"

"I have never heard of it being otherwise," Elda said, "although I have met very few others. Only males seeking mates, whom I avoided after I had met Baru's father, and my own mother, although that seems an incredibly long time ago. I cannot tell you how many of us there are, or where they might be."

"Then there is really no reason why we shouldn't live our lives as we wish," Baru said, "and not lead such solitary existences."

"My own mother told me how things were done, and I never questioned her knowledge, but I agree that our lives would be more pleasant with the companionship of others like us. If it were up to me, I would say let us try, and if anything dreadful comes of it, we can always go back to the way things were. In the meantime, any knowledge I may have is free for your asking." With that, Elda moved over to the little hearth and began blowing up the coals to start a fire for lunch.

Baru interrupted her once again. "Mother, you said you were searching for my father. Can you tell me his name?"

"Dear son, I named you with his name in mind, in case you ever met. He was called Daru, and I have never heard anyone else using a name like his."

Auran had moved over to the fire and she heated up some root broth while they were talking. Now the aroma made them realize they were very hungry, and they were glad to stop and eat.

Later, Roda came to the burrow full of questions about the bearing and raising of children. Baru excused himself and went outside to work on the stone barricade. It had a long way to go before it would serve as protection, but it made him feel more comfortable to know he was helping to build it. Sani joined him and the two of them made visible progress, piling stones that were too small to be of use in building in convenient places to be used for defense, as Baru had suggested. While they were busy, Baru had the feeling they were being watched. He looked around but there was no one to be seen. He went back to his work, but the feeling continued, and he whispered to Sani, "Do you feel as though there is someone watching us?"

"I am not sure," Sani said, "but it never hurts to be cautious. If we face in opposite directions, no one can creep up on us without being seen."

They did so, and after a little time, Sani nudged Baru. "I think I saw something move behind the berry bush over there."

Baru looked quickly.

The bush parted and a male stranger stepped out from behind it. He seemed almost as worn as Elda, and Baru wondered if he too was suffering from the problems of growing older. They stood silently watching each other, and finally the stranger spoke. "I mean you no harm. I have been searching for someone, and if she is not here I will go on my way."

"Who are you looking for?" Baru asked.

"A female who was my mate a long time ago," the stranger answered. "I regretted our parting, but was never able to find her again."

Excitement built in Baru as he asked, "What was her name?"

"Elda."

"What is your name?"

"Daru."

"Then she is here, and you are my father whom I have never seen!"

They were close enough to the burrow entrance for their voices to be overheard. There was a rush of soft footsteps as Auran and Roda came outside, followed by Elda, who was overcome at the sight of Daru. She fell to the ground, unconscious. Auran rushed in to get water, and after sprinkling a little on Elda's face, managed to revive her and help her to her feet.

"Elda, is it really you?"

"It is, but I am no longer the young female you chose as a mate. You have waited too long to find me."

Both had tears in their eyes as Daru took her hands and pulled Elda close to him. "It does not matter. We are together again and this is a fine son you have raised for us."

Elda turned to the others. "Will you excuse us, we have so much to discuss. We have been apart so long."

They moved off into the woods, and the others went to their own burrows. Later they returned as Auran and Baru were having their evening meal. Auran had prepared extra food for them. Both looked very happy, and had regained at least a shadow of their lost youth. After supper, Baru took down his flute and asked if Daru would like to take part in their evening music. He smiled and pulled a flute very much like Baru's from his shoulder pouch. The little group assembled at the entrance, joined by Sani and Roda, and played as Baru had never heard before. He was not yet Daru's equal in music, but he had come a long way. The others fell silent and listened with pleasure as father and son played what was in their hearts. At last they became tired and stopped, and the others began to ask questions.

Auran said, "This is the first time I have ever heard of someone reuniting with both parents. I am so happy for you."

"Now that you have found us, will you stay here?" Baru asked.

Daru replied, "I will stay at least to see my grandchild arrive, and then it will be up to Elda. I will go wherever she wants to go."

Elda moved closer to him, saying softly that she was happier than she had ever been, and with Daru's help she would like to prepare a small burrow nearby, and live out whatever portion of life remained to her with her children and her new friends. No one objected, and they retired to their own places, full of contentment and looking forward to the future.

Between the Mist and the Sun

Chris Romero

The mist pouring through the window blended with the steam rising from the bowl in Darío's black-furred hand. It condensed on the mountain bear's inky pelt and ginger face markings, making them shine in the dawn's hazy light. It penetrated his coarse brown clothes and sandy ruana and he felt its cold embrace as if it were a ghost. It rolled through the kitchen where his wife peeled potatoes and dumped them into the bubbling clay pot above the open hearth. And it finally trickled out the front door of their earth and stone house, covering the front door steps where, once upon a distant time of golden sunlight and eternal birdsong, the old couple said goodbye to their son for the last time.

Staring at the misty window, the male bear took another sip of his hot beverage: a brew of panela sugar with wild blackberries and lemongrass. The sweet, herbal taste with a touch of acidity sent a warm current through his body that awakened him from his morning slumber. He sighed in satisfaction. Then, as happens so often when there's nothing to say, he stated the obvious: "There's a lot of mist today."

His wife dumped another potato in the pot. "It was a cold night."

"Yes." Darío took another sip, arriving at the syrupy bottom. "But the sun is coming up, Alba. The mist will be gone soon."

"Thank Am." Alba grabbed a handful of whole parsley and chopped spring onions, added them to the soup, and dusted off her padded hands. She shuffled to her husband's side and leaned against his taller form.

The mist cleared up gradually; the blurry light turned from cool gray to a burning orange. Soon, dark mountaintops could be seen looming from the haze, crowned by the sun's halo. There was barely enough mist left to look at it comfortably. Darío and Alba went to their knees and offered their traditional morning prayer to Am, grateful for their god bringing light to the world. They prayed silently, heads bowed to the sun, clawed hands folded over their broad chests. There was no need for words: over the course of their shared lives, they had learned to feel each other's thoughts, and so shared their silent prayers, mentally singing the same hymns at the same time. When they stood and opened their eyes, the mist had gone almost completely, revealing the world beyond their window.

Behind their potato plots grew trees with tiny leaves and knobbly twigs plastered with lichens and moss. All over the peaty ground were small, round shrubs, consisting mostly of concentric leaves arranged in a rosebud pattern. But most distinctive of all were the many *Espeletia* plants, standing proud and tall like eternal soldiers. Their shapes vaguely resembled palm trees—woody stems with leaves sprouting from the top, appearing solid silver because of the dewdrops trapped in their tiny hairs. They were the defining feature of the Anasturan highlands: a place forgotten by time, where ghosts of ancient conquerors and warriors could be heard on the whispers of the wind. Darío knew them well. His son's memory often spoke from the mist.

"Let's eat, husband," said Alba. "We have to get everything ready today."

"When are we leaving?" asked Darío.

"As soon as we're done with work." She headed to the kitchen and he followed. As he sat down on an ancient wooden stool, darkened and softened by age, she served dollops of potato soup into two clay bowls. She gave him his soup, complete with a bent metal spoon, and sat down next to him with her own. They whispered a prayer of gratitude and started spooning at the starchy and salty broth.

"It's good," said Darío halfway through his bowl.

Alba managed a tiny smile. "I put a lot of potatoes in it. All the little ones too small to sell."

"Those are the tastiest."

"Yes. But the people don't know that."

His spoon rasped against the bowl. "Mm-hmm."

The sun had evaporated all the mist by the time they were done, yet the morning chill remained in the crisp air. Darío left the house to clean their plates and pots in a small stone basin next to the house, fed by a tiny stream that seemed to spawn from the black soil. Steamy clouds rose from his wide snout as he scrubbed the starch away with a coarse rag.

Meanwhile, Alba took to inspecting their potato plants; they were growing nice and healthy. By the very back of their land, close to the edge of the forest, were her most special plants, carefully grown for longer than the others, specially for this occasion. She bent down, stroked one of the plant's bright green leaves, and ripped it from the ground. A perfect and dirty potato, as large as her hand, swung from the roots. She smiled and the wrinkles under her black pelt deepened.

Alba laid down the plant and walked to the the forest at the opposite end of their land, toward something that resembled an enormous brown rock shaped like a half sphere, covered with a mess of ropes, ladders, saddles, gourds and bags haphazardly tied to its coarse surface. She banged her fist against its side. "Up!" she called. "Up, Rose! Up! Up!"

The great thing shuddered and the ground trembled. An armored tail slipped from its back and its head came out the front, its large, sleepy eyes blinking dumbly. The enormous armadillo was about to go back to sleep when Alba scratched at its fuzzy, unprotected cheeks. Rose groaned happily and slowly stood up on four heavy legs as Alba stroked her enormous head.

"Now, Rose, you need to be well awake. We have a long road ahead." Alba noticed that Darío was done with the dishes. "Husband! Do we have food for Rose?"

"There's some old potatoes and roots and weeds over there." He cocked his head at a large bag leaning against the side of the house. "If you want, I'll feed her and pull out some potatoes while you finish the ruanas."

Alba headed to the basin. Rose made the slightest attempt to follow her, but Alba stopped her with a sharp "Shush!" As Alba retrieved the clean plates and wares, Darío brought the feed bag to Rose, struggling over the farm plots. Rose showed her excitement by swinging her enormous tail, sending little rocks and heaps of dirt flying. Darío plopped down the heavy bag with a sigh of relief and the enormous beast stuck her head inside to chew at the mushy potatoes and wilting weeds.

Alba made her way to their shared bedroom: a small space beside the house, separated from the rest by a doorway in the naked stone walls. Next to the door stood a loom draped in white and red wool threads. Alba sat down on a small stool before it and threw a proud glance at the pile of ruanas in a corner. They were mostly white, decorated with lines of dark geometric shapes along their middles and necks. Today, Alba was to finish the last ruana before the trip. She made sure the red threads were being properly interleaved with the whites, then started to weave. After a few moments, however, she turned to a table next to their large straw bed, no longer able to ignore the piece of wood on top of it. It had been carved carefully and painfully into the familiar face of a mountain bear. She looked at its hollow eyes and took a deep breath. "My son," she sighed, "it's almost over."

Darío petted Rose's head roughly yet affectionately as the armadillo finished eating. He then took one of the bags tied to her carapace and went to their special plot. He tore out the potatoes from the roots with the efficiency of a machine and, little by little, the bag grew heavy.

Time passed. Alba trimmed off the rough edges of the ruana and placed it on an improvised hanger. Satisfied with the quality of the weave and its design—a square spiral sun beaming over black mountains—she took a prickly dried twig and scrubbed at the wool to soften it. When she was finished, she folded the ruana and laid it on top of the pile. She dusted her hands and went to help Darío harvest the potatoes; by the time they were finished the midday sun already loomed over them, the azure sky shining bright and cold.

Alba asked: "Are we done, husband?"

"I believe so." Darío laid his hands on his knees and stared out at the mountains. "We have to leave now or we won't reach town before nightfall."

"Then let's go." Alba stood up. "We change our clothes and we leave."

"Is everything ready?"

"I think so."

"The ruanas?"

"I need to pack them and put them on Rose."

"Mm-hmm," he mumbled and stood up with a sigh. "And what

about..."

"It's right here." Alba showed him the satchel slung over her middle, heavy with the wooden effigy she had fetched from the bedroom and wrapped up in white cloth. "I would never forget it."

"I know." Her partner nodded slowly.

Darío was soon climbing the short rope ladder up Rose's side as Alba fastened the wrapped ruanas behind the makeshift saddle; both of them had replaced their battered and dirty everyday clothes with clean linen robes covered by Alba's white ruanas, and old ribboned hats shadowed their round black ears. Alba stretched a hand to her husband, helping him mount the saddle beside her, and handed him the reins. With a tug from the leash, Rose left their house behind, walking down a narrow dirt path, heavy bags swinging side to side as her riders prayed for a safe travel and safe return.

Alba looked back to watch their humble home disappear at the turn of the road. "Husband?" She hooked her arm around his. "Remember what my cousin told us? About the raiders in black cloaks? That happened in a town very far from here, right?"

"Yes." Darío's steely voice couldn't hide the worry in his eyes. "Yes, it did, Alba."

She grabbed him tighter. "Nothing will happen."

"Am is with us." He squeezed her hand in reassurance. "Nothing will happen."

The couple watched the terrain change as they descended toward the town. Healthy oaks and conifers appeared amidst the bush. Bright green vegetation with large leaves, longer stems and brighter flowers replaced the drabber colors of the highlands. The *Espeletias* seemed to disappear from one moment to the next, and soon the hills around them were decked in patches of grassland and crops. Occasional huts could be seen here and there, most of them devoid of any life despite appearing well kept.

"Everyone must be in Tamaraziga already," Darío remarked after passing a familiar household.

After a few hours they saw a small wooden stand by the side of the road, flanked by an enormous clay pot over a bed of dying embers. A young tiger cat boy stood by it, accompanied by his mom. They both wore similar outfits to Darío and Alba: long boots, linen robes, ruana and hat. The spotted felines waved happily at the couple as they approached.

The young mother spoke first. "Good afternoon Darío, good afternoon Alba! I was beginning to think you wouldn't come down this year."

Darío tugged at the reins and Rose stopped beside the stand with a mighty snort. He and Alba returned the friendly wave. "Good to see you, Hope!" Darío said, smiling. Alba added: "Ligio, you're growing more and more every time I see you!" The feline boy giggled in pride and the male bear looked back at Hope. "You know we don't miss the burning festival for anything," he said.

"You're right," she said. "Come down! The tamales are still warm. Son, go inside, get us some blackberry juice."

Ligio took off with a joyful sprint. Meanwhile, Darío handed the reigns to Alba as he carefully climbed the ladder down Rose's shell. On the last step he misjudged the distance and almost fell, but Hope got his shoulder at the last moment. "Careful!" she said, half joking, half worried.

Darío huffed. "The years are starting to weigh on me."

"Nonsense." The tiger cat looked up. "Need help, Alba?"

"Yes," replied Alba. "Tie her up somewhere, will you?"

Hope led the titanic armadillo to a tall oak next to her stand and tied her to the tree with the ease of someone who had lived a whole life working the field. Alba waited patiently until Rose had settled next to the oak, then she climbed down the ladder and went with the rest of the little group. Hope was busy prodding the submerged tamales with a wooden stick, Darío was hungrily looking over her shoulder, and Ligio was jogging back from the house with a hefty, dented metal pitcher and wooden cups, spilling drops of rich purple juice in the process.

Hope lifted a hefty tamal bound in palm leaves and knotted with string, passed her stick below the knot, fished it up and put it on a slab of clay on her stand; the smell of fresh dough, starchy water and cooked leaves rose with dainty wisps of steam. Darío and Alba's stomachs grumbled in return. They hadn't had anything but water since the potato soup for breakfast.

"Ligio, serve up the juice. Our friends must be starving," said Hope, fishing up a second tamal.

"How much, Hope?" asked Alba, about to reach into a pocket of her tunic.

The female cat raised an eyebrow. "You have money on you?"

"Not much," Darío chuckled nervously. "But we can trade you some potatoes for the tamales."

Hope mused for a moment and said, "Twenty-five potatoes for a tamale."

Darío's eyes went wide. "You're killing us!"

"My tamales have chicken. Chickens are expensive to raise."

"I can give you twelve," the bear said, and Alba had to hold back from rolling her eyes.

The feline grinned at the challenge. "Twenty-two."

"Fourteen."

"Twenty."

"Sixteen."

"Nineteen."

Darío crossed his thick arms. "Am be blessed, you will leave us nothing to sell. Seventeen."

"Seventeen," Hope chuckled, and they shook hands happily.

Alba and Darío ate with glee. As promised, the tamales contained generous amounts of chicken, but also boiled eggs, rice, fried onion and tomatoes and even bell peppers. Hope's tamales had earned their reputation amongst the local farmers and it showed; the bears had to hold back from munching on the greasy palm leaves they had been wrapped in. They talked about the usual things as they ate: the weather, the crops, who had gotten sick, who had moved out, and, of course, the festival, and how many people were coming down, and, Am almighty, poor Ani's mother had passed away, although it was to be expected, of course, she was very old, but she looked so well, and how was Ani doing? As they ate, Ligio answered the call for play from some other boys down the road—another tiger cat like him, a mountain bear and a brown mouse—and scampered away with a little smile and wave.

After trading in the potatoes and drinking up the sweet juice, both husband and wife had to resist the pleasant lethargy of a full belly. For a while they shared a comfortable silence with Hope, despite the pressing knowledge of passing time and they not being in sight of Tamarazigá yet. Then, Hope made sure her son wasn't around and asked in a whisper, "You're going to burn him, right?"

Alba's dark eyes opened in surprise, then looked down with pain. "Yes." Darío lowered his head; his hat's brim shadowed his gaze.

The feline looked aside. "It's difficult, isn't it?"

"How did it feel?" Darío asked, not raising his head. "When you burned Ligio's father?"

"Painful," replied Hope, still looking away, at something only she could see. "Very painful. But also...freeing. You feel a weight leaving your body. You realize you've set him free. You did a good thing. Then the emptiness sets in, but you learn to live with it."

Silence. The couple absorbed those words, tasted them, analyzed them, and found solace in them. "Thank you," Alba whispered.

Hope looked back with a soft smile. "Of course." A small pause. Her smile disappeared when she pursed her dark lips. "May I...If it's okay..." She sighed. "Can I see him? Just to say goodbye?"

Darío looked at Alba, who was already putting a hand in her satchel. She pulled out the wrapped piece of wood and, with care and reverence, took off its cloth wrapping. Hope gasped as she looked at the ursine face of the totem. Then, slowly, tentatively, put a hand over it, as if caressing it. "Goodbye, Etan. Rest well amongst the stars."

A black and pink dusk caught up with the travelers. Rose marched on carefully, flanked by a steep hill on one side and a steeper drop on the other, whilst Darío and Alba, exhausted and worried, began to wonder if they would reach town before nightfall. Pebbles rolled down with each heavy step of the armadillo; the naked dirt and stones of the scarred hill betrayed recent landslides. Darío and Alba did what they always did when worried: they held hands and prayed in unison.

They rounded a curve and saw a cluster of orange lights between the trees. They were close to town.

They left the winding hills a few minutes later. The dirt path widened into a pebbled road, which led into the town of Tamaraziga. Houses of whitewashed adobe and cobblestone stood on both sides of the road, lit up by warm candlelight that poured out over chipped and mossy window frames. They waved at the shy children of different species peeking at them from the windows and some waved back.

The pebbled road turned into a stone street when they entered the town proper. "Husband," Alba started, "it's too late to go to the center of town, isn't it?"

Darío could only muster a tired, "Mm-hmm."

"Want to go right away to my cousin's house?"

"Yes," he sighed. "Let's do that. They must be wondering where we are."

With a tug of the reins Rose turned down a narrow side street barely wide enough for her to shuffle through. Strips of contiguous houses stood on either side of the steep climb like walls; bromeliads and grasses grew from rooftiles of ancient terracotta. By now night was truly upon them, and the milky black sky, with infinite stars alongside the waxing moon, muted the world's color and tarnished everything with the gray sheen of old silver.

Close to the end of the street, where it tapered off into a tiny path into the woods, was a house with a heavy door of carved wood that may have been green once. Some candlelight managed to slip out the closed windows through the cracks of their wooden panels. Here Darío tugged Rose to a stop and Alba climbed down the ladder and knocked on the door.

Almost immediately a square peephole above a handle opened, and a brown eye surrounded by black fur with white marks looked at Alba with surprise and then reproach. The old hinges of the door swung open with a pained groan, revealing a female mountain bear, just shorter than Alba, silhouetted against the fiery glow of candles and a chimney from the house. A coarse white veil, draped over her neck and disappearing below her ruana, could not hide the many flashes of gray hairs in her black fur.

With a sour face, she nagged in her crackly old voice: "Cousin Alba! Where have you been?! You took so long! We were worried sick! What happened to you?!" Then she threw her arms around Alba with a big smile of relief.

Alba returned the smile and embrace. "It's good to see you, cousin Filomena."

"Oooooh, yes, it is!" Filomena nearly squeezed the air out of Alba, then she released her and looked at Darío, still perched on top of a slumbering Rose. "What are you doing up there, old bear! Get down! Tom will take care of your armadillo. Tom!" she shouted, turning around. "Tommy! Come down here! Say hello to your aunt and uncle!"

There was some slipping, some tripping, some running noises, and out came a lanky young bear, taller than the rest, wearing a loose-fitting linen robe and sandals of rough interwoven fibers. The older teen gave a half-forced hug to Alba and said awkwardly, "Hi aunt, hi uncle." He turned around to head back inside, when Filomena caught him by his flappy sleeve.

"Tomas..." She cocked her head at Rose. "Go tie up their armadillo to some tree up there, will you?" It wasn't a question.

Tom looked at Filomena helplessly, then at Alba, then at Darío, then back at Filomena; he was about to say something but it fell apart in a sigh of resignation.

"Hello Tom," Darío said brightly, trying to win back his grace, even as he tossed him the reins. He climbed down Rose's shell with some effort and set foot on land with a little grunt—the weight of the years again—while Tom led Rose away. Darío had barely turned toward the house when Filomena struck him with a hearty hug.

"Come in, brother-in-law, come on in," she insisted, shoving him inside after Alba.

The house's white, uneven walls glowed amber with the light from the fireplace crackling to their left, enriching the air with the fragrant scent of burnt eucalyptus. A little doorway to the right led to a kitchen with an iron stove blackened by grease and time yet lit up by generous candlelight, contrasting with the two dark rooms looming beyond the warm fire. Mosses and tiny ferns looked down at them from the moist rafters, while the smooth stone floor did little to warm up the cold house.

Darío looked back at the door for a moment. When he turned around Filomena stood in front of him with mugs of steaming panela water and buns of sweet brown bread. He noticed Alba already sitting down next to a little table by the stove.

"Ready to eat, brother-in-law?" asked Filomena.

Darío replied: "Mm-hmm."

"Then come! Now! Come, come!" And the old bear shuffled back the way she had come.

They sat around the table on little wooden stools that, somehow, didn't break under their bulk, exchanged how's-it-goings and questions on relatives and ancient friends. Tom entered the house a few minutes later. He tried to snatch some bread and leave, but his mother dragged him down and forced him to listen passively to the talking of old animals.

First Filomena asked about the farm and the crops—a repetition of Hope's questioning. Darío and Alba said the morning frost killed some crops a week or two ago, but other than that, they were managing. Then they spoke about the trip. Hope's tamales. Yes, very delicious, Filomena agreed. The rolling pebbles by the hill at the entrance. Filomena shook her head. Landslide. Road just got cleared in time for the festival. Who cleared it? The church soldiers, of course, Am bless them; Father Celestine oversaw everything. And how was Father Celestine?

Then Darío asked about Earnest. Filomena's old eyes, always so bright and alert, grew gray. Tom was about to doze off, but his father's name woke him with anxiousness and an odd sense of violated intimacy. *What do you know? What do you care?*

Filomena explained. No letters. No news. How long? Two months. Alba tried to cheer her up. No news usually means good news. But then she hurt herself with her own memories of letters and missing sons.

She remembered the morning she and Darío received the news of Etan's death, nearly a year ago. They had woken up for breakfast, shivering with unusual cold, their breath turning to crystal powder around their potato soup. Then, piercing the sacred silence, came a fast and rhythmic gallop of talons on dirt. Darío and she rushed out of their house. The morning frost had stripped the dawn of color, turning everything gray and cold. Just by the start of the dirt road to town, close to Rose's sleeping spot, was the sight they had hoped never to see: a sad little mouse riding an ostrich with bags of letters tied around its wings. The dark mouse wore pure white robes that fluttered as fallen leaves in the wind. His bone-colored hood obscured his eyes.

At the edge of the crops, he climbed down his mount and walked to the expecting couple.

Alba's next memories were a blur. But the one thing she remembered the most was the pain. The searing, tearing, piercing spear that ripped through her heart and left her airless and weak. She cried, Darío cried, and even the faceless mouse clenched his teeth and fists in sympathy.

It was Hope who first visited them after hearing the rumors of Etan's death from passing clientele. The tiger cat rode her ostrich to the highlands and found a house shrouded in decay. The couple hadn't eaten in a week. They rarely rose from their stools, and when they did, they shuffled like the living dead. Little weeds had started to crowd their crops and Rose was moody and shifty with hunger.

Hope managed to convince them that the pain would not leave unless they found closure. Since Etan's body could not be given a proper cremation as tradition demanded, they did what so many other families sharing their fate, including Hope, had done: they carved an effigy in resemblance of their deceased loved one, and waited until the burning festival to burn it in lieu of the missing body. Then, according to the church, the deceased could rest in peace as if properly cremated.

Alba gripped the satchel a little tighter. Filomena's words brought her back to the present: "Do you think we will live to see the end of this war, cousin?"

Without raising her head, Alba whispered: "No."

Bugs chirped in the distance. The burning twigs cracked. Tomas cleared his throat and said, "I'm going to sleep."

"Yes," Darío grunted, "Let's all go to bed. Tomorrow'll be a long day. Thank you for everything, Filomena."

The old bear smiled. "Of course!"

She gave them a lit candle and extra blankets for the night. Then she extinguished the stove and went to her bedroom alongside her grandson, just after Darío and Alba had taken off their travel clothes and crawled under the heavy blankets.

The couple woke up well after sunrise to the distant sound of drums and flutes and cheering. The four bears shared a hearty breakfast—potato and chicken broth, eggs with tomatoes and spring onion, more of that sweet brown bread and panela water—put on their robes and ruanas and hats, and left the house, leaving only Tomas behind.

After a few minutes, Darío, Alba and Filomena were riding on top of Rose toward the center of Tamaraziga. Children of different species whooped and ran around them, awed at the size of the armadillo and the bags of potatoes swinging from her sides—a few even managed to snatch a potato or two.

Darío, with reins in hand, turned to Filomena and asked: "I don't see a lot of festival goers."

"They're all in town square already," she replied, holding her hat as a gust of wind blew over them. "Most people set shop yesterday. You're the ones who are late, cousin-in-law!"

The street broadened as they approached the town square, and the bubbling murmur of many voices, alongside the melodies of pan flutes and drums, rose in volume. The small, contiguous houses became two story estates, with ornate wooden balconies from which hung flowerpots containing vivid orchids and carnations of all colors.

They saw an open space bustling with animals beyond the next block of houses: the town square. The wide streets surrounding the square were filled with animals, ostriches, armadillos, and giant sloths. Farmers, artisans, medicine men, and all kinds of sellers occupied the sidewalks with flimsy wooden stands selling everything: potatoes and corn by the sack, stones glimmering green with raw emeralds, candied guava and dragonfruit, and tobacco chew for headaches and height sickness. At the far end of the square, to the right of the bears, stood the town's church. The T-shaped building consisted of the entrance and main room stretching out at the front, twin buildings connected at the back, and a tower at the intersection of the T, proudly showcasing a four-pointed white star against a backdrop of dark olive mountains. Above the busy streets stretched enormous arches made of thick bamboo stalks, from which hung offerings to Am brought by animals far and wide. Fat trouts, chickens, turkeys, even pieces of ostriches; bananas, mangoes, papaya and aloe vera tied up in strings; small bags of potatoes, flour, corn, barley, beans, rye; bundles of flowers of unimaginable variety and beauty, and clothes, and kitchenware, and anything and everything one needed to live, suspended in the air as offerings to the sun.

The three bears had to bow their heads to avoid crashing into the offerings. A black jaguar with fine leather clothes pushed his way through the crowd and yelled at them excitedly: "How much for your armadillo?!"

"She's not for sale!" Alba replied, loud and clear.

"I'll give you good money! Above market price!"

"No, no! Can't do, mister! Sorry!" Alba smiled. "She's part of the family!"

The jaguar sulked away and the bears made their way through the crowd. Rose approached another armadillo and let out a short, high-pitched call, and the other beast grunted lowly in response.

Darío tugged at the reins. "Not now, girl. We got to sell our stuff first before making friends."

"Darío!" said Filomena, shaking his shoulder to get his attention. "I have some friends on this side of the fair that have a ruana stand. Alba and I can go sell your ruanas there. They charge us nothing for the place. Sounds good?"

"Mm-hmm," replied Darío. "Need help?"

"It's fine, husband," Alba said, already untying the bundle of ruanas. "You stay with Rose and sell the potatoes. Find someone to hang those big ones, alright?"

Darío nodded and kept Rose in place as Filomena climbed down the armadillo's back. The older bear held out her hands and Alba threw the bundle of ruanas to her. As soon as Filomena caught them, she climbed down to her side. "See you later, husband! May Am watch over you." Alba waved at her husband, then helped Filomena carry the bundle into the crowd. Darío barely had time to answer the wave before he lost them both amongst the sea of animals.

Darío led Rose to a spot that hadn't been occupied yet, close to the opposite side of the square. Darío was soon selling his potatoes to passersby who all tried to haggle him into dirt-cheap prices, while Rose snored happily next to him.

Hours passed. Animals came and went. The sacks of potatoes slowly but surely grew lighter. After some asking, Darío found a young mouse who would string up the special potatoes for a few coins. The bear paid him and the youth ran away, then returned with a makeshift bamboo ladder and a couple of friends. By the time the mice had finished hanging the heavy sack, the sun had already risen to its zenith and the church bells began to ring. Darío turned to the sound, not believing how time flew by. Was it truly midday already?

The excited murmurs that rose from the crowd cleared his doubts. Some animals on the opposite end of the square got on their knees, heads bowed and arms folded over their chests, as the church's dark wooden doors opened slowly. Darío squinted to see. The figure that stepped out was tall and elegant, adorned with silky robes of iridescent white that glowed under the sun and contrasted elegantly with his black wolf's head. Darío felt a warm joy at the sight of Father Celestine; he folded his hands over his chest and went on his knees, just like all the other animals around him. It was time for the middle hour prayer.

When the square had grown silent and everyone was on their knees, the wolf raised his clawed hands to the sky. "May Am be with us!" His raspy, commanding voice carried the hint of an old accent.

As reply, the whole square chorused: "May it be so!"

Father Celestine smiled; an honest, serious smile, belonging to a kind yet strict parent. He closed his eyes and raised his head to the sun. "Almighty Am, creator of everything and everyone, we raise our voices to thank you for your blessings and guidance. May it be so!"

"May it be so," answered the crowd.

"On this special day, we humbly ask you to take our meager offerings in good faith. Moreover, we ask you to give rest to our loved ones, those who on this day we remember and wish to bid farewell to. May you take them into your grace and allow them to live with you in eternal peace as stars in the sky. May it be so."

Even whilst on opposite sides of the square, Alba and Darío felt the same bittersweet hurt in their chest at the same time. "May it be so," they replied somberly, their voices lost in the chorus around them.

"Now, let us pray."

At this, the priest went on his knees like the rest of his following. Everyone stretched out their arms and raised their closed eyes to the sun, attempting to catch as much light pouring down on them as possible. Basking in the warmth of the sun and the sacred silence, each animal raised their heart's voice to Am, the Creator, traveling the sky in the shape of the sun directly over them.

The peace was shattered by a distant and unseen woman's cry, ragged and tired and panicked, fast approaching, panting, running: *"Raid! Raid! The blackcoats are coming! The blackcoats—!"*

There were nervous murmurs and rumbles as a collective fear seized hold of the animals. They opened their eyes, torn out of their reverie, and looked around nervously, wondering if others had heard the same thing. Had it been only a bad joke? A false alarm?

No.

Shrill screams rang out from all directions, getting louder as the sound of heavy, fast galloping grew near. High-pitched, bestial roars accompanied the terrified screaming of animals. Darío's blood turned to ice.

Panic erupted as a two-legged beast stormed out of a street on the far end of the square, close to the church. The avian predator rushing to the congregation ran on two powerful legs, its talons longer and sharper than war daggers, its black-dyed wings close to its sides, its enormous curved beak open to release piercing shrieks. It was a kelenken—a dangerous beast used only in combat. But to most of its victims, it carried a more descriptive name: terror bird.

Riding the beast was a female figure cloaked in black up to the ears. With her face darkened by a hood, the only clue to her species was the brown, vulpine tail behind her. She tugged the reins, stopping her mount by a corner of the square filled with petrified animals, and raised a long rapier along with a shout of ire and might: *"Death to the church!"*

Another tug of the reins, another piercing cry from her terror bird, and she tore around the square, slicing through the bags of offerings hanging from the bamboo arches with her rapier, sending grain and dust flying.

Wild screams and stamping in all directions followed. Father Celestine and his acolytes ran into the church and closed the doors in a frenzy. Feeling himself drowning in the smells and sounds of chaos and fleeing animals, Darío looked around through hazy eyes, thinking only of one thing: finding his wife. Another blackcoat rider had appeared. Then another. And another. Four, five, six riders cloaked in black wrought havoc through the streets and the square, tearing through the arches and offerings, through the stalls and sacks and animals in their way—tearing through everything, even the wailing screams.

"Help! Help!"

"Mamma! I'm scared! Mamma!"

"Am save us!"

"Where are the soldiers?!"

"Husband?!"

Darío's round ears perked at the sound. He turned to its direction. Was it real? Imagination? He saw nothing but dark flashes of terror birds and stampeding animals and beasts. Rose groaned in panic, quickly hiding her head in her shell until she looked like a giant rock.

"Husband!"

There. To the other side of the square. Darío let himself be led to the sound, even as animals crashed into him, even as the terror birds rushed and ripped and screeched all around. "Alba!" he screamed above it all, "Alba! Alba!"

Close to the edge of the square, Alba heard his distant voice. She turned to Filomena crouching under the stand with ruanas next to her, hiding from it all, fervently whispering prayers and clutching her hands on her chest. "Cousin!" Alba tugged at Filomena's shoulder. "Come! We have to go!"

Paralyzed, Filomena replied shakily, "Y-Yes...Yes..." She snapped herself out of her fear with a hearty shake of her head. "Yes! Where's my cousin-in-law?"

"I'm going for him! You go home! Now!"

Filomena looked at Alba with doubt. "Cousin, I can't leave—"

"I'm getting Darío and then I'll follow after you," Alba assured. "Go! Please!"

The older bear stood up and hugged her cousin for a moment. Then, as fast as her body could muster, she jogged back into the street they had come down, alongside a group of animals.

After a small sigh of relief, Alba made her way to Darío's yells. Then came a loud, bestial wail. She turned. A giant sloth, still carrying its saddle, came running at her bleeding from its flank; a kelenken and its rider followed close behind. Alba jumped out of the way, landed on the ground, and immediately felt the weight of the stampede on her, kicking, pushing, hurting, stepping. She covered her head and growled in pain as someone kicked her sides and arms. A moment later came a reprieve in the flow of animals. She took her chance and stood up, only to smash into a larger mountain bear that almost put her down again.

She collected herself and looked around. The crowd had grown thinner and she saw Darío immediately. Their eyes met. Their legs stumbled; they walked, then ran to each other, even as her whole body ached from the blows of the stampede and his throat hurt from ceaseless yelling.

Then they were in front of each other, and shared a brief, strong hug, warm relief making them forget the terror and pain for just a moment. Alba felt tears welling in her eyes and broke the hug. She looked up at her husband, and his dark, glistening eyes, and smiled. Darío did the same. And then Alba felt the absence of a familiar weight around her middle. Her smile vanished in panic as she stuck a hand in her satchel.

It was empty.

The couple shared the same incredulous expression as a frenzied Alba patted herself all around. Her dark furry face wrinkled and twisted in anguish. "I f-fell," she recalled. "I fell a-and—"

Darío grabbed her shoulder and stared into her reddened eyes. "Where?!" he demanded at the verge of tears.

She turned around to look at the place, but found nothing and no one. The square was empty of everyone but themselves; even Rose had scampered off in the chaos. The only ones remaining, besides them, were the four kelenkens slowly approaching, snapping their beaks hungrily as their cloaked riders stared down at them with shadowy faces.

They both felt it at the same time: the dizzying, sinking feeling of their hearts dropping from the chests to their stomachs, turning their bodies into ice statues and pricking their skins with a million invisible needles. The feeling of impending doom.

Darío turned to the church. A kelenken was trying to break open the heavy wooden door with its beak, screeching at it while its rider spurred it on with furious orders.

Darío pressed himself against his wife and put his hands into hers. They whispered a desperate prayer together as a blackcoat rider made its way to them, exuding a different aura from the rest of his companions. His kelenken was covered in a fine mesh of dark metal, decorated with geometric shapes painted in bloody crimson. Thick chains were wrapped across the rider's burly frame, rustling with each slow step of his mount, partially covering those same red symbols stitched into his black tunic. Long ears protruded from the top of his hood, and when he cocked his head at the two bears, they finally saw the patchy chestnut fur and brown eyes of his lapine face.

He raised his hand to reveal the totem wrapped in dirtied bandages. Alba stifled a cry and Darío felt himself prisoner in a surreal nightmare.

The rabbit smirked at the terror in their faces. He stopped his kelenken in front of the two bears; its shadow covered them both. "Do you want it?" he teased in a juvenile voice—he was little more than a teenager.

Darío and Alba shivered silently in response.

"You believers are so pathetic. Treating a piece of wood like this." The rider tossed the totem up and down as his companions watched. "I asked…" His teasing voice lowered to a dangerous growl, "Do you want it?!"

It took a moment for a terrified Alba to croak out, "Y-Yes."

"Then beg for it." The rabbit looked down expectantly. "Come on. On your knees. Beg me for it, you ignorant believers."

The pained couple looked at each other and, with heavy reluctance, went down on shaky knees.

One of the other blackcoats guided his mount close to the rabbit: the brown vixen who had sliced through the offerings. "Gustaf," she hissed, "cut it out."

Ignoring her, Gustaf carried on. "You can do better." The rabbit jerked down his arm and twisted his wrist; a long piece of his chain unwrapped from his arm and slid down smoothly between his fingers as if it were an obedient snake. He whipped the chains at the ground in front of the bears with a violent crack, sending tiny pieces of stone flying in the air. Alba started sobbing with a yelp, and Darío held her close in a tight embrace, believing it to be the last one they would ever have.

"*Beg me for it!*" Gustaf spat. "Beg me for it like you do to your imaginary god!"

Something cold went through Darío. He felt himself someone else when he answered, "No."

The rabbit cocked his head in mock surprise. "No?"

"No," the bear carried on. "You're not Am. You're not a god. You're just a killer. I will not sin by worshiping you."

Another smirk. "How right you are, old bear. Then you can die first."

Gustaf lifted his chains for a killer blow, brown eyes filled with murderous intent. Alba cried out and wrapped her husband in her arms. Darío closed his eyes and prayed and waited for the blow.

Instead, he heard a surprised remark from the rabbit: "What are you doing, Naila?!"

Darío opened his eyes and saw him and his wife nearly under another kelenken. He looked up. The brown vixen had put her mount between Gustaf and them. "You're being petulant, Gustaf," she said.

The rabbit clenched his teeth. "My father put me in command of this raid! Stand aside!"

"And your father ordered me to make sure you followed his orders." Naila spoke calmly, coldly. She straightened her stand. "No killing unarmed civilians. Not now. We're hunting clergy."

"Tshk." Gustaf looked down at the totem in his arms. His ears straightened in alert to the sound of approaching gallops and cheering.

The blackcoat rider assaulting the church's door, which now had a hole in it the size of a head surrounded by jagged splinters, returned to the group. His spotted yellow feline tail curled in annoyance behind him. "Soldiers!" he announced, voice shaking. "Lots of them, by the sound."

Silence. The group looked expectantly at Naila, who in turn glared at Gustaf. "Petulant child," she muttered.

The rabbit glared back.

"Let's go!" the vixen commanded. "There are other priests to kill."

Naila led her kelenken to a side street and the other blackcoats followed, except for Gustaf, who looked down at the incredulous bears with disdain. He spat at the totem and tossed it away like trash, before following the rest of the group out of the square.

Not one minute later other kelenkens ran into the square, ridden by animals in chainmail and chest plates covered with short white capes and etched with silver-white insignias of four-pointed stars. They found Alba and Darío huddled on the ground, crouched over the wooden effigy, crying on each other's shoulders. The square had been ransacked; most offerings lay strewn around on the ground, some arches had been bent or broken, and the stalls and their contents had been thrown down.

A couple of soldiers approached the bears. One of them—a slim cougar—slid off his kelenken and walked to them. "What happened?"

he asked.

Alba sobbed: "A miracle. A miracle just happened."

Another soldier, this time a well-built mountain bear, climbed off his mount and approached the couple with less grace. He stared at the couple as recognition and surprise lit up his face. "Aunt Alba?" he gasped, "Uncle Darío?"

Darío looked at the soldier, equally amazed. "Earnest!" he smiled, "Earnest! You have your mother worried sick!"

It took a long while and all of Darío and Alba's combined strength to pull Filomena away from her son, after she had nearly choked him to death with hugs and sobs. Tomas followed his mother to the square, and his cold façade broke in tears when he saw his father's scarred face and felt his sinewy arms embracing him. Animals and beasts slowly returned after a few soldiers made sure the blackcoats were all chased from the town. Eventually, Rose found her way to the square, following other armadillos, and received many hugs and sweet words and caresses from Alba and Darío, before being nagged for running away. It was late afternoon by the time everyone had laughed and cried and talked themselves into calm, and a cool wind began to flow down from the dark mountains behind the church.

The family of bears stood huddled together by what used to be a ruana stand. Alba's work had been trampled and stained by the stampede. "What a shame," she remarked. "We barely sold a couple."

"I'm sorry you had to go through all that, aunt Alba," said Earnest, standing next to his son.

"Don't worry, nephew," she said with a smile of resignation.

"It's Am's will," Darío continued. "We will manage. We always have." And he put his hand on her shoulder, while she clutched the totem in her satchel.

She sighed. "I've seen mothers and fathers go into the church with their own carvings. I think..."

Darío nodded. "Yes. It's time."

Alba commanded Rose to stay put, and the family walked to the church. Soldiers with swords and bucklers stood guard next to its defaced entrance and bowed down their heads in reverence when they noticed the clothed wood in Alba's hand. There had been many mothers in the same position, preparing themselves to burn away their effigies. Far too many.

The church was simple and austere. Off-gray adobe walls with their wooden pillars under a roof of darkened wood, too far up to be touched by the glows of the candles next to the pews. A fireplace surrounded by glass panels crackled at the far end of the church, right at the base of the tower, beside a simple stone altar. The bears recognized some of the townsfolk staring at the fire, praying to the representation of Am on Earth, and wondered who they were praying for.

Darío and Alba grabbed each other's hands as they walked to the fire, followed by Filomena, Earnest and Tomas. Father Celestine stood next to the cracking fire, wishing strength to a crying female ocelot. The couple fought their tears as they approached, and the wooden totem felt as heavy as lead to Alba.

With final words of sympathy, Father Celestine bid farewell to the ocelot, then turned to the couple. His yellow eyes, mellow but tired, closed in pain. "I was wondering when you would arrive, old friends," he said, his voice rasped. "His name was Etan Bernal, right?"

"Yes, Father," replied Darío. "Yes, it was."

"He was a good child." The wolf sighed. "Do you need a moment to say goodbye?"

"Please," Alba whispered in return.

Father Celestine nodded solemnly.

Alba unfolded the cloth wrappings and looked at her son's wooden face for the last time. "Goodbye, my child," she whispered, tears streaming down her face. "Rest easy. Rest well. We will see each other sooner than later."

Darío caressed the carved wood behind the ears, just like he did when his Etan was a baby. How he enjoyed it. How he laughed. How he smiled. He choked on the memories. "My son..." A single tear slipped from his closed eyes. "My son. We will see you amongst the stars."

Silence. Nothing but the cracking of the burning fire, its light reflecting in their fresh tears. With a shaky sigh, Alba handled the effigy to Father Celestine. The wolf looked down at the wooden totem, then turned to the family of bears. "Rejoice, old friends. Your son has not been able to rest. But now, he will be free. He has died for the church. He has died for Am. His honor and place among the stars are assured for all eternity."

Darío nodded in understanding, holding Alba close. Father Celestine approached the fireplace. He knelt down in front of it, raised the totem above the glass panes, and let it fall into the burning wood.

The couple felt the hurt at the same time—the reopening of a badly healed wound, followed by a cleansing burn. The emptiness Hope had warned them of loomed above them, but higher still was the promise of peace for the dead and the living.

Darío and Alba saw the glowing embers rising from the fire, burning up into the fine smoke that ascended into the air alongside their son's memory, through the tower directly above them, slipping alongside the quiet bells, past the terracotta roof, riding the breeze from the mountain, and becoming one with the pure air between the misty mountains and the setting sun.

The Wind Howls, the Willows Weep

Stephen Howard

"But why Mole, eh? What harm did he ever do anyone?" Ratty exclaimed, leaping up from his perch by the alcove window.

Badger, unusually reticent, merely nodded. He sank further into his armchair, gazing into the crackling fire, the silver streaks in his fur shimmering in the light. Mole was, Badger thoroughly agreed, the best of them, which made his death and its nature so darn hard to swallow.

As he stared into the flames, he swore they licked up into a vague shape: the face of Mole! Badger removed his spectacles and rubbed away the smudges. When he replaced them, the face was gone.

"Badger? You look like you've seen a ghost," Ratty said, collapsing into the adjacent armchair.

"Hush with such talk, there are no such things as ghosts. Anyway, you know full well who is responsible for his death."

Ratty webbed his fingers together and grimaced. "Toad is a lot of things, but—"

"He's been cavorting with the weasels again, frequenting their taverns." Badger leant forward in his chair and stared over his spectacles.

"You know better than to listen to Owl's gossip," Ratty replied.

Badger coughed, beating his chest. "Toad hasn't been the same since he was forced to sell Toad Hall and those darn motorcars. And I do not indulge in gossip."

"Toad may live by a different code, but he's never been anything less than honest. Too honest, occasionally. Now, will you help me in my enquiries? The local law seem content to write off Mole's death as a tragic accident, but you know as well as I he would never have taken to the river alone."

"Squirrel is a lazy sergeant. I ought to speak with his mother... Okay. But you must remember we are not young whippersnappers anymore," Badger said.

Ratty shrugged his shoulders, then nodded.

Rain lashed against the windowpane and a storm started up in a hurry.

Ratty leapt from his seat once again. "Oh gosh, Badger, on my life, did you see it? Did you see that face in the window?"

Before Badger could respond, Ratty ran to the door and yanked it open, allowing the storm to billow in and blow about the papers on Badger's writing desk. Ratty stuck his head out and glanced side to side, seeking out what he'd seen. He called out, though the wind swallowed his voice.

There was no response.

But then came something to tickle Ratty's eardrums. A faint whistling sound, distinct from the wind, which sought to entice him further out into the storm.

Badger pulled Ratty back inside and shoved the door closed. He locked it and turned back to his old friend.

"You'll have to stay the night, Ratty, there's nothing for it."

"But, Badger, it was him. It was Mole, I'm sure of it." Ratty stumbled backwards, hands on his head.

"No such unnatural business occurs, Ratty. I'll go make up the spare bed. I suggest you pour us each a finger or two of whiskey; we've unsettled ourselves with all this mystery and death." Badger slumped off to retrieve his second set of sheets and blankets.

Ratty stood by the window, trying to make out anything in the seemingly impenetrable dark, but the trees had merged with it to form an opaque mass. What had that whistling been? A flash of lightning illuminated the woods, the trees bits of string shredding in the storm.

Darkness again.

Badger returned. "It will pass by tomorrow."

Ratty nodded. "Good. There are things we must settle."

It lingered above the cottage. A presence of uncertain, wavering density, seemingly real and unreal all at once.

The presence could see only in vague shapes and pastel colours. Some of the shapes were familiar. The smells and the sounds too.

Something drew the presence to this place; some strange energy powered its existence.

It lingered.

As predicted, the storm had passed by morning, leaving the forest trails sodden and slippery. Ratty and Badger traversed these trails with care, Badger employing his walking stick to steady himself. His once-muscular bulk was crooked, and he bent forward with each step. Ratty remained lean and trim, though the walk soon saw him breathing heavily.

They found the road and caught a bus into town, knowing Toad rented a room above Ye Olde Cock Inn. Badger didn't care for anything with an engine, but accepted his legs weren't what they used to be. Before long, they were sitting in a corner booth of a quaint village pub awaiting Toad, for whom they had sent. A smell of roasted chestnuts and apple cider clung to the air.

"My old chums! How are you scallywags?" The unmistakeable voice of Toad burst forth from the stairway, whereupon he appeared with a spring in his step. Wearing a smart, expensive tweed suit and flat cap, he gestured to Tom Otter behind the bar for a drink and declared it be added to his tab.

He settled on a stool and Badger regarded him with his observant eyes. Up close, the suit hung from Toad's thin, stringy form, and dark arches propped up eyes that refused to rest on any one thing, instead flitting from corner to corner as if in expectation of some strange sight.

His skin was dry. A sure sign of ill health in a toad.

"Well, not in the best of spirits, Toad. Naturally," Ratty said, raising his glass.

The others followed suit, clinking their ales.

"Of course, of course. Poor, dear old Mole, what a tragedy! I was so deeply sorry to miss his funeral. Urgent business took me away from town, I'm sure you understand," Toad said, not looking up from his glass.

"Committing an animal back to the land from which it came is a sacred thing." Badger heaved a deep sigh, swallowing anything further on the subject, but he'd made his feelings clear. They sat in silence, save for Toad's leg bouncing beneath the table. They listened intently to the chugging of a motorcar along the street outside, the whistling of wind slipping in between the pub's old wooden beams. A cold draught tickled their ankles.

"We're actually on something of a quest, Toad, and wondered if you might help your old pals out?" Ratty said, puncturing the silence.

Toad stiffened and fiddled with his bowtie using those long, green fingers. He shook his head and answered. "Well, yes, of course, anything for you chaps."

Badger and Ratty exchanged a glance. In the background, Tom Otter shuffled about collecting glasses, the glass chinking with each addition to the tower in his arms.

"Go ahead, Ratty," Badger said.

"We are treating Mole's death as suspicious, Toad, and we're trying to retrace his steps. What brought him to the river that day? Now I recall Mole saying he was to visit you that very morning. Did he seem off to you, or did you notice anything unusual?"

Toad tugged at his collar and glanced over his shoulder. "No, Mole didn't see me that morning. Perhaps he'd meant to, but hadn't got so far? I really don't think I can help you chaps after all. In fact, I've got some business this afternoon, so I'll have to make tracks shortly. You know how it is."

"We don't, Toad. Why not enlighten us? Business with whom?" Badger asked, crossing his thick arms.

"It's all a bit cloak and dagger until any announcements can be made, you see. But let me assure you it'll have me back on my feet before you know it!" Toad said, waggling a finger, a flash of his old pizzazz surfacing.

Toad leapt from his chair, which overturned and clattered upon the floor. "Which of you grabbed me?" he shouted, head twisting this way and that as if in some desperate search.

Badger and Ratty shook their heads.

Toad dusted his overlarge suit off. "Gosh, must have been the draught, felt like someone wrapped a paw around my ankle. Silly me. Golly, look at the time. I really must be off."

"We're going to visit Mole's grave tomorrow, drop off some flowers. Perhaps you'd like to join us?" Badger asked in a slow, deliberate tone.

"Flowers? It's not really...I mean, they'll only wither and die. And anyway, I've got a business meeting, so I can't. No, I'm sorry, I simply can't. It was good to see you chaps, look after yourselves." Toad tipped his cap and skittered out of the bar area as if being chased by a hound.

Badger turned to a crestfallen Ratty, eyebrows raised.

"I really thought he'd come with us tomorrow," Ratty said.

Badger stood quite suddenly and stomped over to the bar. "Tom, on Tuesday three weeks past, did good old Moley pop in to see Toad?"

Tom stopped shining the glass in his hand and stared upwards, deep in thought. "Tuesday...Aye, he did. I 'appen to remember because they crossed some stern words."

Badger nodded solemnly. "Did they leave together?"

Tom stared upwards once more. "Aye, they did."

Badger turned back to Ratty and raised his walking stick. "Finish that ale quick-sharp, we've got to follow that blasted Toad."

The door opened and the one in the suit scurried through it. The presence felt a rising animosity, some smell or aura pushing forth a memory. Nearly a clean memory. An unhappy memory.

The presence knew it had some dastardly connection to this creature. It swooped through the open door in pursuit.

Badger and Ratty pushed through the pub door and glanced left and right, but there was no sign of Toad. Shadows coated the narrow street as the cold winter sun shone brightly above them.

"Wait, up that way!" Ratty said, pointing past Badger's snout.

Before Badger could locate the source of Ratty's exclamation, he heard a giant rumbling sound, felt those dreaded reverberations through the cobbles. The noise grew louder until the motorcar appeared like some grim yet shiny spectre. It flew past them, whipping their coats up like a dust storm, screeching to an abrupt halt further down the road. Its door sprang open. From a little alley emerged a skinny fellow in a tweed suit.

Toad entered the vehicle. No sooner had he shut the door behind him than the engine roared and transported him from sight.

"Did you catch the license plate, Ratty?" Badger muttered, adjusting his flat cap.

"I'm afraid to say I did," Ratty replied, rubbing at his eyes.

"It seems Owl's idle gossip was more accurate than you gave credit for," Badger said.

Ratty nodded slowly. "There could well be some innocent explanation for all of this, you know. This is Toad we're talking about! He's no doubt got into his head some silly moneymaking scheme and thinks Mr Weasel will loan him some sort of start-up cash."

"Mr Weasel is not in the habit of fraternising with legitimate businesses." Badger grunted, then nodded to the bus stop. "It's bad enough I'm forced to ride these eyesores, but increasingly I am subjected to the hideous roar and foul oil smell of motorcars. We animals are straying further from our roots. Soon, we'll be no better than humans."

Ratty sighed as Badger stomped off towards the bus stop. His old friend's temper would get the better of him one day, and he feared for his ailing health. Though Badger would never admit it, he was half the beast he'd been when they'd raided Toad Hall and rid it of its squatting scum.

Ratty daren't ask whether Badger saw something follow Toad into the car. The wispy sight of something he couldn't quite describe or explain...

It had chilled him to the bone.

Badger called back for Ratty to hurry up, a call to which he quickly obliged.

The hedge maze stood quiet and resolute to their left as they wandered up to that most familiar of halls. If they'd stopped to listen intently, they'd have heard a whispering voice chasing round its puzzling paths, as if someone had lost their way.

But Badger and Ratty marched onwards. Toad Hall looked as tall and proud as it had when Toad owned it, but instead of his family's heirlooms and memories it now housed nefarious activities, the vices of gamblers and carousers, the music of cursed troubadours. When once its wings were wide and welcoming, the whole place seemed to be a sinkhole into which one might fall and never climb out.

Mr Weasel's motorcar was parked out front.

Ratty and Badger nodded to each other and pushed open the thick double doors.

Music and laughter assailed them. Not sweet music and generous laughter, but songs with a bitter edge and laughter more like uncontrolled squeals. It smelled like a brewery on fire. Badger and Ratty shuddered simultaneously.

To the left was a bar area rammed with ferrets, rats, and weasels, all clinking glasses and arguing loudly with each other. There were even a scattering of humans indulging themselves: a rare sight. To the right were the roulette and card tables, despite such activities being banned if actual money was gambled. Smoke hovered like rainclouds. Sat at one of the tables was Squirrel, the local policeman, which explained the blind eye being turned to the nightly activities here at Toad Hall. Badger shook his head in disdain.

"There, Toad's old study!" Ratty said in a hushed, excited tone.

Sure enough, towards the back of the gambling area was Toad being unceremoniously bundled into his former study. A weasel pulled the door shut and stood outside, back straight, eyes narrowed.

"The shame of it all," Badger muttered. "Come on."

They felt the eyes of the weasel pass over them like the scorching rays of the sun, but his attentions soon turned to the drunken ferret showing off a handful of chips he'd won at the tables.

"To the back corridor," Badger said, eyes fixed straight ahead.

They passed beyond the deafening din of the business area, then the wide gothic staircase, skipped beyond a red velvet rope, and found themselves in the corridor behind the study. With a bit of luck, they could eavesdrop on any conversation from the back door.

Sure enough, fingers of light crept beneath the door. Ratty held up a hand and, gently, slowly, eased the latch off and the door open, only an inch or so.

A gravelly voice slipped through the gap.

"You're looking tired, Toad. Things weighing heavily on your mind, are they?"

Toad started to speak, but spluttered and coughed, then cleared his throat of phlegm. "I've not been sleeping so well. Accustomed to rather a different standard of living, as it were. But never mind that, I have identified a new source for our business—"

"Our business?" the raspy voice interjected.

"I, um, sorry, I mean of course your business, for which I hope my rather sizeable investment will prove useful and, erm, fruitful." Toad's voice jumped an octave higher.

"Precisely. Your friend. I assume we can expect no further... meddling?"

we were such good friends, once, the four of us

Ratty jumped and turned back to Badger, thinking it was he who had whispered in his ear. Ratty's elbow caught the door, pushing it open.

A concerned voice shouted from the study.

"Darn it. Badger, go, go!" Ratty hissed.

They scurried along the varnished floorboards, dodged the velvet rope, and passed the stairs. The music grew with every step and as they reached the bright lights of the bar area, the weasel who'd stood watch at the study door stepped around the corner, arms crossed, a scowl on his whiskered face.

"Who are you?" he growled.

"Got lost, old chap, looking for the bathrooms," Ratty said, affecting an exaggerated glance around the place. "My friend here thought he'd got a dust mite in his eye and needed to wash it, being a gentleman of poor sight, but in our hurry we got ourselves somewhat lost."

The weasel looked them up and down with a sneer. "I suggest you leave our establishment now, else we'll give you more to worry about than a speck of dust."

Ratty felt Badger stiffen behind him and deftly placed himself in the space between them and the weasel. For an animal who'd warned him they were no longer 'young whippersnappers', Badger seemed more energetic than he had in years.

"We were just leaving," Ratty said.

They traipsed up the road towards the bus stop. Darkness fell all around them, offering the jagged outline of the trees across the road a sinister cloak.

"You really made me jump back there, Badger. What was it you said? We all used to be friends?"

"I didn't say a thing. You spooked yourself, no doubt." Badger fell a step behind Ratty, placing greater weight on his walking stick. "You should have let me whip that snivelling weasel. Don't think I didn't see what you did there."

Ratty laughed but said nothing more. He watched the shadowy outlines of the trees and mulled over the snippet of conversation they'd caught back at Toad Hall. Toad was in over his head with these nefarious characters, of that he was sure, but what did he mean about a meddling friend? Surely not Mole? Surely not.

They reached the glow of the oil lamp beside the bus stop. The rustling of leaves and bramble could be heard from beside the road, sounds Ratty would once have had no doubt in identifying. Now, in the midst of their investigation, surrounded by strange occurrences, he couldn't help but speculate these noises were something mysterious and creeping, something malevolent.

Badger stared up the road, a statue, stolid, uncompromising. Cold breath clouded around him.

"Someone said something, Badger," Ratty whispered. "There's a mystery here beyond that which we are seeking to understand."

Badger sighed, his gaze unwavering, as he searched for headlights. "There is no mystery left here, Ratty, only a decision to be made."

"A decision? Oh Badger, you are a much less patient fellow these days. We must give this due thought!"

"These days, Ratty, I feel greatly inclined towards action because we live in a world of bystanders. Our woodlands and fields are shrinking to make way for smoke, for grey buildings, for the pollution of our quiet homes. When we were young, we knew where we stood. We knew everyone in the villages and we trusted them. Now, you have these nefarious types roaring through our streets, conducting their vile business in the halls of our oldest families. So yes, Ratty, I am less patient these days. That I am. I see a serious wrong has been committed by someone we once called friend, under the malign influence of a criminal. I will not stand for it."

Two yellow lights, like good old Owl's eyes, appeared in the distance.

Badger reminded Ratty of a poem he'd read years ago during his school days. He knew his friend would not go gentle into that good night. His friend was rage, and he would resist the dying of the light with every scrap of his remaining energies.

"Let's sleep on it, at least," Ratty said, a hopeful note in his voice.

The presence followed the two familiar voices out onto the winding country roads, and joined them in some bright, loud form of transportation. It smelled foul, but the presence tolerated it.

The outlines of the two figures had become clearer. The presence knew these two, knew they had been friends. Good friends, even.

They were going to get themselves into trouble.

The presence wished it could warn them somehow. It tried to will itself into physical being, hovering beside the two figures, only for them to waft a flailing hand as if a fly were buzzing about their person.

This simply would not do.

Ratty slept in Badger's spare bedroom once again, having been offered it until this sordid business was at an end. Light poured in through a gap in the curtains. It was late morning.

Voices carried through from the living room and Ratty dressed in a hurry, meandering through somewhat groggily.

"Ah, Ratty, dear Ratty, I thought I'd find you here!"

Toad stood beside the bookcase, as if keeping as much distance between himself and Badger, ensconced in his armchair, as possible. The room was bright, the curtains wide open with the ropes knotted through the tiebacks. Tea and biscuits were on the table, steam rising from the pot in little swirls.

Sitting down in the opposite armchair, Ratty surveyed the sorry, ragged figure before him and couldn't help but pity the poor creature. This was their chance to hear him out. "What have you done, Toad?"

An unusual cold passed Ratty by, as if from a draught, but it came and went in seconds. He reached for his tea to warm himself up, only to notice the steam from the pot splitting and escaping upwards in two separate columns, as if an invisible hand were placed above it. Ratty rubbed his tired eyes. The pot appeared normal again.

Toad, having paid no heed to Ratty's hesitation, instead focusing on the barely concealed sneer upon Badger's face, began.

"Well, I've really gone and gotten myself into a scrape this time. I invested all my remaining money in a scheme run by a respectable local businessman—"

"Enough of your petty squabbles and prevaricating, Toad! What really happened to Mole?" Badger rose in one rapid movement that belied his rickety limbs and glared at Toad, who jumped and plastered himself to the wall in fright. Books tumbled from the shelf. Toad squealed.

"Now Badger, sit yourself down before you do yourself a mischief. Toad, old boy, it really is time you tell us the truth. For old time's sake. You owe us, and Mole, that much." Ratty's voice had a distant quality. He remained seated, eyes still focused on the teapot resting upon the low table.

Toad shrank into himself, deflated, as if the idea that had propelled him to Badger's abode had escaped him at precisely the wrong moment. "But...but Mr Weasel, he's paranoid, you see, totally crazy! I know Mole went to see him, you see, though I don't know what about. It wouldn't surprise me if he had something to do with Mole—"

A preternatural wind rushed through the room. The curtains flung shut, yanking the tieback pins from the wall in an eruption of dirt and plaster. They hit the floor with a dull thump. Silence. Three pairs of wide eyes searched for some sign of the happening's origin, but they found nothing, no small creature zipping around, no troupe of malign actors; it was instead some invisible hand once again.

he's lying

Ratty leapt up from his seat and tumbled into Badger, who heaved deeply, but grasped his friend and righted him.

"That voice..." Ratty whispered.

Ratty dived forwards to check behind the armchair. He found nothing. Glancing back at Badger, a tightness in his chest, his eyes were then drawn to the absence of Toad.

The door was open.

Toad had scarpered.

The presence sensed its growing strength. In that moment, in the home of its old friend, it had nearly pushed on through to their side and relayed its message with clarity. Nearly.

It had remained there even as the light outside dimmed and died. Only then did one of the home's occupants depart. The larger of his two friends ventured out into the woods and veered from the beaten path, cutting through marshy land and bumpy terrain with a singular, plodding certainty, and a near-visceral anger. He did so alone. He walked with an aid, with a stick.

The presence followed.

His friend entered a tunnel and the air smelled familiar. Yes, they had entered this tunnel together once before, but there had been four of them then, when their bonds of friendship were at their strongest. Oh, his friend had been quite the fearsome creature back then. He was not so anymore.

On his friend pushed, his form bent and shivering, until a light ahead beckoned. As his friend passed from the tunnel and into the light, his bent form contorted further, and his cries echoed back through the claustrophobic space from which he'd come. The presence panicked, felt its grip on this plane slip, as if all its focus was needed to maintain this feeble form it had mustered. Into the light it went, only to see its friend assailed by several sinewy creatures holding batons and clubs.

The presence could do nothing.

Another figure entered the room, a booming, scratchy voice passing through the veil with a facetious menace.

You think I wouldn't have the tunnels watched? You think I'm a fool, that us weasels have short memories? We know you. We know you well.

The presence lingered.

Toss him back out into the tunnel, fellas. Let him rot.

The presence fled.

It was the branch scratching at the glass that woke Ratty. All around him the cloying hand of darkness created moving shadows, the dim light of the moon piercing any gaps it could find in the curtains.

Ratty's eyes adjusted.

A face hovered just above him. A faint outline glimmered, much like moonlight but also not, somehow less certain. A determination existed in this outline, as if it were a weak signal struggling to maintain itself, struggling to push through the ether and reach its destination.

the tunnel

Ratty couldn't move. The voice was hoarse, but he understood it.

our friend, pain

Ratty blinked, tried to force the bedsheets from his prone figure, but invisible shackles held him down. The outline grew stronger, the features of its face sharper, bolder. An odour assailed Ratty, one of moisture and dirt, the type you'd find in a deep, dark place.

go to him now, before it's too late

As quickly as the figure had appeared, it was gone, and Ratty flung the bedding from himself in a fit of desperate activity. He pulled open the curtains and looked about the room. Nothing else revealed itself.

"Badger!" Ratty exclaimed, rushing from the room and bursting into Badger's quarters.

His bed was empty.

"Where the devil could he..." Ratty trailed off. The words began to make sense to him, pieces of a puzzle slowly revealing a bigger picture. Ratty gasped and threw a hand to his mouth, feeling only now he fully comprehended the strange cold that had followed him, the flashes of images he'd convinced himself were overactivity of the imagination; they were in fact his friend reaching out from some otherworldly plane of existence.

Mole had come to warn him.

Ratty threw on his clothes, boots, jacket, and cap, grabbed one of Badger's spare sticks, and set off into the night.

Mrs Hedgehog mopped Badger's sweaty brow and pushed a mug of water beneath his snout, insisting he drink from it in small, consistent sips.

Ratty watched from the doorway. His tail skittered around his legs as if restless.

"It's a wonder he's alive, Ratty. Who could have done such a thing to dear old Badger? If he wasn't such a tough old so-and-so, with the constitution of an ox, I dread to think..." Mrs Hedgehog shook her head and trailed off into a small whimper, her needles softly sagging.

"There are some nefarious types wandering our forests these days, I'm afraid to say. It was sheer luck I stumbled upon him when I did, and luckier still Owl was on hand to fetch you. He's gone down to the police station to report this, naturally, though I suspect nothing much can be done," Ratty replied. Of course, luck had little to do with it. He'd called upon Owl on his way to the tunnel entrance and claimed Badger was missing—which was hardly untrue, in a sense—whereupon the two of them had set out together. Upon finding Badger and dragging him back from the tunnel, he'd sent Owl off to fetch Mrs Hedgehog, knowing full well her nursing skills were unparalleled in their neck of the woods.

Talk of ghosts of dead friends and their timely warnings, he omitted.

Ratty turned and poked at the fire, then set another log upon it. The cold had followed them home and infiltrated Badger's abode with a singular thirst, a thirst only a fire could sate.

"Well, I should hope that layabout Squirrel does his job and apprehends the culprits!" Mrs Hedgehog declared. She spooned small amounts of soup into Badger's mouth. He was awake, though only just. His head was bandaged, as were his hands. He'd been in quite a dreadful state when they'd found him.

Ratty sighed. He poked the fire once more, hoping to stir something within the flames, to bring about the face of Mole, to see that friendly visage once again. Nothing appeared.

Mrs Hedgehog soon agreed to stay the night, though she concluded Badger was through the worst of it and his injuries would heal in time. Ratty nodded along with a wry smile, knowing full well Badger would look to cut down his so-called recovery time as much as physically possible. Stubborn, that's what he was, and that's why he'd snuck out and left Ratty asleep in bed. Thinking he could tackle Mr Weasel's men alone. Heck, the two of them together would be no match for the young, battle-hardened brutes employed by that most despicable of creatures. Their business was unnatural for animals of these parts. Some malign human element had caught fire with them, their vices becoming the animals' vices. Ratty shuddered.

And where was Toad? Surely he had nothing to do with this? Ratty found his faith in his old friend wavering like a candle set upon the sill of an open window.

He said goodnight to Mrs Hedgehog and a drowsy Badger, then retired to his room. Tomorrow, there was someone he needed to visit.

Ratty heard the rumble of cars from the big motorway they'd opened recently. A frightful din. He marched onwards, deeper into the woods, until the trees thinned and the horrible sound of roaring exhausts was replaced by the lovely rushing of a river. The clouds above threatened rain but were holding firm.

Ratty reached the riverbank and it sounded of home. White Willows lined the way. Their leaves were speckled silvery, little clusters of constellations among a green sky. Ratty breathed in the air. He stared down into the dark blue—this stretch was fast-flowing, powerful—and saw the shadows of pike darting along like little spears. He watched the branches and debris bob along on the surface and smiled.

He held a small bouquet of pansies in his hand.

A sniffling sound disturbed his reverie, and he glanced along the bank. Someone stood just inside the tree line. They were stood right by Mole's grave.

Ratty wandered in that direction. As he closed the distance, he saw the tweed suit and the worn old flat cap. Shoulders slumped, head bowed, Toad leant over Mole's grave, staring at the headstone, whimpering. A chill wind bristled Ratty's whiskers, reminding him of a friendly gesture he used to give Mole, tickling him beneath the chin.

"Not dropping off flowers, are you, Toad? They'll only die, after all." Ratty passed Toad and placed the bouquet across the mound of earth. Around the grave, the willow trees sagged as if they too were mourning.

"I didn't expect—" Toad began, but Ratty interjected.

"What happened to us, Toad? You avoid us, your eyes flit about as if expecting ghosts to jump out at you from around every corner. You missed Mole's funeral." Ratty slipped his hands into his pockets.

"I've had a busy time of it, is all," Toad replied. His face was lined and weary, his eyes red and watery.

"I always defended you, you know? When Badger would wax lyrical about your misadventures, about your fall from grace, I would always say you were an honest chap. A foolish one, perhaps, but honest and good at heart. Was I wrong, Toad? Was I wrong to defend you?" The sky darkened as the first drop of rain fell. A rumble of distant thunder rolled towards them like the spine of some dreaded sea creature breaching the surface of the water.

Toad dropped to his knees, unable to take his eyes from Mole's headstone. The headstone had a simple inscription.

Here lies Mole.

A good soul, a great friend.

Ratty and Badger had been pleased with that. Mole was a simple soul for which only a simple epitaph was needed, and it was these words upon which Toad fixated.

Until he rose suddenly.

"He should never have got involved!" Toad shouted, flinging his arms out, his suit so loose it might fall off him.

"Involved in what, Toad?" Ratty asked.

Rain fell harder, its rapid pitter patter swelling the river below .

Toad, eyes shining despite the dim light, stepped towards Ratty. Ratty could finally see what Badger had seen all this time; the jovial, good-natured Toad they had once known was gone, lost to his wicked schemes and wicked associates.

"Mole dogged my footsteps for months. He warned me about Mr Weasel, said no good could come from dealings with him. But I knew what I was doing. Mole just refused to see that the old ways were dying out, that business required a new type of thinking, a modern way. In the end, Mole followed me one step too far and he was becoming too troublesome for my business partner, sticking his nose in where it didn't belong..." Toad glanced over his shoulder, swiping at something Ratty couldn't see, and turned back to him.

"I knew Mole wouldn't take to the river alone," Ratty said.

A shadow fell across Toad's face. "You know, I thought you wouldn't question that part."

He shoved into Ratty with such force as to knock him off his feet. Landing in the mud of the riverbank path, Toad leapt upon Ratty, grasping at him, wrestling with the wild strength of the desperate. Ratty flapped and shoved the flailing Toad away.

"Stop this Toad, we can work this out!" Ratty cried.

"I don't need your help!" Toad yelled above the rumbling thunder. Lightning flashed and illuminated the wood. In that brief moment of brightness, Ratty saw the outline of a faint figure hovering above them.

leave him alone

A voice carried quietly on the wind, but Toad, in his madness, continued to struggle with Ratty.

leave him, Toad, haven't you done enough?

Louder now, firmer, a full voice. Toad went still. Ratty shoved him off his chest and rolled over, struggling to his feet.

"No, I can't hear you. You don't exist. You're gone, dead, the past." Toad scrambled up and threw punches left and right, grasping at thin air, all the while shouting curses and spilling forth terrible wails. He stepped backwards, towards the edge.

"Toad!" Ratty reached out a hand, but Toad slipped and was gone.

Ratty crouched down, clasping his hands together. Tears welled in his eyes. He felt a strange cold beside him and knew that, though Toad had been swept away by the river, he was still not alone in this place.

"I thought I could help him, Moley, old chap, I truly did. And I know you did too. That's the kind of friend you were. I think perhaps whatever is happening now, it's time you found a little peace. And don't worry, I'll keep this little escapade between us. Badger would never believe me anyway." Ratty chuckled to himself and wiped away a tear.

The strange cold faded like the passing of a storm. The rain slowed to a stop and the clouds broke, the shy sun peeking through.

Ratty gazed at the bright light and smiled.

It took a visit from a fully recuperated Badger to Squirrel's mother, and their combined efforts to cajole a few contacts with connections to the big city, before the raid of Toad Hall could be organised. With the evidence of Mr Weasel's vast smuggling operation collected, the city police put him away for rather a long time, along with a host of his cronies, including Squirrel, for his deliberate negligence.

It had taken two glasses of whiskey for Badger to admit the big city types weren't all bad.

The two old friends sat in camping chairs beside Mole's grave. They revelled in the warmth of the spring sun and the earthy smell of the woods, all the while listening to birdsong and the soothing sounds of the river.

"Do you think he escaped?" Ratty asked for the hundredth time.

"For a Toad, he wasn't the best of swimmers," Badger replied. His wounds had healed fully, and, somewhat miraculously, his stubborn and angry spirit had soothed. If Ratty had known it would only take a good clip around the ear to calm his old friend, he'd have done it himself years ago.

"No, no. I'm afraid he rather wasn't."

The two sat together without speaking for some time. They drank in the natural world around them. They mourned Mole, for he was a good friend and a good animal, but they mourned Toad too. Not what he became, but the roguish friend they'd once known.

"No creature should go unburied," Badger said hoarsely.

Ratty nodded. The old ways were important to Badger. They were important to him, too, and he secretly wondered whether some disturbance in these ways could cause an animal's spirit to become trapped in-between, just as Mole's had been.

These thoughts passed.

He ruminated further on his friends.

Years ago, they'd taken back the overrun Toad Hall, united by that common cause and by friendship. Ratty remembered those days fondly. Wherever he found himself now, Ratty hoped good old Mole was feeling settled and safe, remembering the good times they'd had too.

Whalesong

Laki

Between the wavering fronds of seaweed, beneath white speckles of plankton in the moonlight, a seam line opened in the sea. Swirling vapors poured forth from the infinitesimal gaps between water and salt, then pulled apart to reveal an oblong window to the stars. All around the world, from the sunniest coral reefs to the yawning chasms of the shadowy deep, gateways were unsealing. They appeared in each of the many sacred places that marked the beginning and end of all great whale pilgrimages, and every kind among the whales, toothed and baleen, made the journey. It was their privilege, responsibility, and sacred gift, upholding the tradition since the dawn of all things to sing their dreamsongs in the astral sea.

Thousands of sleek, graceful bodies flowed through the portals in every corner of the ocean, and for some, it would be the first journey of many. The vast spans of time between entries to the celestial plane were marked by the children born and elders lost, because during the ritual, the two could coexist for a precious moment beyond the boundary of life. Parents and pods started to teach their young not to fear the vibrant, crystal clear abyss as soon as the little ones could remember any stories sung of it, but still, it was such a terrifying wonder to behold. Such open clarity, with not even the haze of life-filled waters to hide behind, was so foreign to the calves. And stranger yet, the dreamlike *nothingness* they swam through, without a single note of resistance, fulfilled the roles of both water and air, giving the gifts of endless breath and limitless access alike. There was no 'surface' or 'beach' to be stopped by here. While many young whales, their eyes and hearts overwhelmed by sparkling paradise, wished to remain for all time, their stay was limited by the inevitable encroachment of need. Catching the spectral fish that occasionally leapt from glittering pools as the travelers passed could amuse the senses, but never fill the belly. And so the amassing pod carried onward in singular purpose through the stars.

One particularly elated little dolphin calf, whose name was Tahn, absorbed absolutely every stray bit of light and color that presented itself to her senses from her mother's side. She knew that these were not the real stars, of course, and that traversing this place was not the same as if one had simply taken flight into the earthly sky. While nighttime above the surf at home was decorated with orderly rows of perfectly equidistant dots, the realm beyond the seams was pure dreamy chaos. Here, the "stars" were countless shattered bits of crystalline light, suspended in clouds of bejeweled dust. From a distance, the collective created impossibly vast, colorful streaks, like kelp leaves so giant that each could cradle the whole world on their own. From up close, all the varied gems—tiny as a grain of sand to as large as a clam—appeared ghostly, mere mirages of steam, and yet they would part and drift off in streaks when nudged by fin or beak.

Tahn was of a sizable dolphin-kind, though one with barely a snout to speak of, and she was fascinated by how all this crystal-like matter could slip along her sides without leaving so much as a scratch. Her own earthy, shale hide was still largely unmarked by the painterly swirls and streaks that decorated her mother. Every bump against stone and run-in with a feisty squid removed the pigment from their kind's skin so completely that her mother's face was utterly white from simply experiencing the necessities of life. Tahn had hoped, briefly, that she might be bequeathed with shooting-star lines as a memento from the journey, but the astral dust was more slippery than sand, more liquid than glass.

When all of whale-kind finally met at a central point, hugged by a puffy, violet-hued tower of cloud, the gathering ballooned into a hollow audience formation, much like a jellyfish's bell. The grandest members took position along the bottom of the sphere, noses tipped upward and tails dangling away into the depths, while the smaller varieties faced inward from the sides, gathered in loose groups with their families. All colors and kinds played neighbors at random to all others throughout the congregation, with one exception. Those of sleekest black, with great white blotches just behind their dark, obscured eyes, took care to remain in a group with their own kind. Their section of the audience stood out starkly due to their faces, the white patches giving them each the appearance of having a shrewd, unblinking stare. Nonetheless, when the collected mass began to raise its voice in song, every whale in attendance joined.

Chipper whistles, longing wails, and accenting clicks grew louder and more cacophonous by the second, each individual member of the choir beginning with a song of their own. These were the songs of their dreams, every one carefully remembered and selected as the favorite of the dreamer who sang it. Only the most beautiful, the most promising, the most enchanting and uplifting would do. With great gusto and passion, every individual sang their heartfelt song, describing their vision and the promise it would bring, and in the course of this, neighbors heard pieces of each other's dreams and were enchanted by them in turn. Gradually, some conceded their song to that of another, persuaded to test the description of the new dream with their own voice.

Personal choirs formed in increasingly homogeneous segments, and none were more surprised by their own power to sway the hearts of others than Tahn. That she was merely a calf did not matter in the spread of her sweet song, no adoptee of her music fully aware of who the original dreamer was. None could be prouder than Tahn's mother to hear the growing synchrony of the nearby crowd with her daughter's song. She was the first to convert, her motherly plan from the start, but the surprise of hearing the volume grow to reach even the wisest giants among the gathered excited her even more than Tahn, for whom full realization had not yet struck.

When only a few songs remained, the original chaos tamed to a sort of multi-piece harmony by consequence, the most venerated of guests arrived to join the Chorus of the Dreamsong. From the starry depths all around emerged the ancestral spirits, great and small, who lingered in the astral to await this very day. They were seen only by their edges, glowing and iridescent, made of the same sparkling dust that seemed to effuse this entire plane. While the living maintained their songs, they couldn't help but glance behind at the beautiful spirits who added their own echoing, ghostly calls to the tunes. The songs had the ancestors' support. There would be no more need to narrow the selections further—these were the ones.

As was the tradition passed down from every generation to the next, the originators of each chosen dream brought their notes upward into a crescendo, made mighty by the multitude and variety of whale voices in their company. Tahn gaped at the enormity of her segment of the choir. All told, the congregation had split their tunes into only a precious three. She could hardly keep the breath in her lungs after the last note, the crushing weight of sacrality suddenly heaped upon her, but when she felt her mother's fin upon her back, she did her best to be at peace. She would need to steady herself and take courage for her next performance—the one to gain final approval by the whole.

The first of the three to come forward, moving to the center of the massive encircling audience, was a rotund baleen whale with an impressive lower jaw and stylish row of barnacle spots. He crooned and reeled with the smooth ease of one long-practiced and full of charm, unhindered by the notion of countless witnesses trained solely on him. The youngest members of the audience, Tahn included, were mystified to see the spectral vision that formed around him from astral dust to reveal visually what the lyrics described.

> *In my dream I see*
> *A sea*
> *Showered by stars in the night*
> *That know no symmetry*
> *They come in assortments*
> *So random and unique*
> *That pictures can be seen*
> *As in clouds*
> *As in dreams*
> *What imagination defines*
> *The memory can keep*
> *This I see*
> *While navigating the sea*

Alongside the performance of his song, promising to scramble the current perfection of the real world's stars, all of whale-kind swayed, tumbled, and rolled in their places to dance. It was a relaxed, serene song, and the movements it inspired flowed to match, from the tiniest calf to the mightiest ancestor. Trails of dense, sparkling light streamed from the ends of every dancer's fins, drew down toward the singer, and wrapped around him and his final whirl of climactic flourish. The streams of astral dust, inspired by the dreamsong and approval dance of the many, condensed before the dreamer into a burning diamond of rainbow flame, about the size of his own heart. Deeply pleased, the whale turned about in the ethereal air to give the newborn star a tail-flick, launching it upward to the open top of the audience bubble.

Having waited on the periphery for their duty to arise, a huge, broad-finned manta ray swooped in to gather the burning promise of a dream upon its back and ferry it ever higher into the astral cloudscape to its ultimate destination. In the end, this dreamstar, and any fellows that joined it, would be dropped from such a height that they would fall from one realm to the next. Out in the physical plane, all the other creatures of the world were waiting, keeping an eye on the heavens above for a sign of the Chorus's completion. Any and every inspired change, new species, and all touchable and intangible things were made real by the dreamsongs of the whales, from the first to the last. Many a breath was held as sea lions, gulls, turtles, pelicans, and every other animal with foresight waited to see what would be made real on this night...

It was time for the second dreamer of the Chorus to come forth. This one was much smaller than the first, a dolphin-kind like Tahn, but spotted and sporting a prominent beak. They wasted no time in breaking into the most gleeful, upbeat of songs, and the vision that coalesced from the astral dust around them was just as vibrant and sunny.

> *In my dream I see*
> *Upon the islands in the sea*
> *A very special kind of tree!*
> *Up high it grows*
> *With fronds all in rows*
> *And toys for you and me!*
> *When the shell turns brown*
> *The fruit will fall down*
> *And float upon the sea!*
> *Entertaining and fun*

A home for some
And a special trick indeed...!
Give it a smack
And if it should crack
You'll get a tasty treat!

Tahn giggled and creaked with delight, imagining so vividly the chance to bop one of these fibrous, funny things with her nose and play toss by flinging it out of the water with her tail. As before, the stardust gathered, pressurized itself into a living jewel before the dreamer, and was sent flying with panache up to the next awaiting manta ray to carry ever higher.

Then it was Tahn's turn. The calf looked to her mother for assurance, and was given a loving nuzzle and pat with a fin to soothe her and send her off. Tahn felt like a shy little fish adrift in the open sea, it was taking so long for her to reach the center of the tremendous space. Glimpsing down, she was stunned for a moment by the unbelievable grandeur of the mightiest, yet gentlest of whales gazing up at her. They were so incredibly far away, and yet their permanently wisened smiles were as clear as if she were looking at a mirror up close. Their slow, kindly blinks and rumbles of approval to encourage her, intermingled with those of their spectral ancestors, felt like the most surreal of dreams.

Prolonged quiet followed Tahn into the starring position. An undercurrent of endeared chittering passed throughout the Chorus as they realized en masse that the wait was for an adorably shy young calf. Fairly certain she was centered enough, Tahn looked around at the audience to grasp who it was that she must sing for—the entire population of whale-kind—and it was a mistake. She could no longer even locate her mother in the distance, and any sound refused to come out. However, her hesitance was met with great patience, and the more energetic dolphin-kinds from her own supporting choir began helpfully reciting the opening portion of the rhythm they remembered.

Thanks to this, Tahn closed her eyes, imagined how beautiful the enchanted image woven by her song would be in the stardust, and did her best to forget the audience and immerse herself once more in the dream. It was simple in composition and scope, but it was hers.

In my dream I see
How land can share its beauty
On soaring cliffs high above
A special gift blooms like love
Tall forests rain petals like rose
Such delightful music for the-

She stopped mid-lyric as she realized a growing uproar from below was not merely in her imagination. As she opened her eyes, the mirage of her telling disintegrated. Ruby trees, swaying in a warm sea breeze along a cliff's edge, broke apart to reveal a surging, deep dark that she could not immediately understand. The blue giants below fled from the intrusion on their space with annoyance, forcing the congregation of whales to shift as a cooperative, single organism. The jellyfish bell of their collective bodies tucked upward and squeezed into itself, but stubbornly refused to move any further. Tahn allowed herself to float toward the nearest wall of her kin for security, unsure whether to be frightened at first. But when she saw the ancestor spirits turn and fade into the increasingly oppressive dark, the wrongness sunk in.

From the inky black below, the single form of a tattered whale emerged. He was big, though only half the size of the true giants his arrival displaced. His swimming was slow, labored by the drag of tarry sand that spilled ceaselessly from his cracked hide and the weight of countless barnacles grown *into* his flesh. Ripped bits from his fins and the streams of grime sank and radiated outward as he rose, and every whale closest to the bottom of the tightening formation scattered and swam higher to avoid it as urgently as death. The once-joyous Chorus was now a racket of cries and whistles hurled at the interloper like rocks, their meanings varied but unified in purpose—*he* was not welcome here.

In the swirling, Tahn found herself closest to a surly narwhal who was glowering and screeching disapproval at the bleak stranger's approach. She squeaked an urgent inquiry song to him over the din.

"Excuse me
If you please
Who is he?"

126

The narwhal eyed her with bewilderment at first, but swiftly understood.

> *"Ah, you're just a sproutling of kelp*
> *Too wee to recall*
> *And, what's worse*
> *Wronged, your dreamsong unspun!*
> *But this naivete will be shared by all the young...*
> *Listen! Listen! Friends near and far!*
> *We must alight the tale once more!*
> *So the calflings understand*
> *What our singing is for!"*

The message spread through the churning mega-pod of whales in a rippling wave, swiftly reaching the furthest of ears and temporarily calming the furor. Then, together, led by the eldest among them, all who knew the tale joined, echoing a recounting of the events that followed the one they despised. It began with every nose pointed directly at the culprit, a rush to the clicks and tones and squeals. His gradual ascent toward them was a threat they did not have long to explain.

> *Him! Him! He was the first!*
> *He was the one who dared to bring*
> *A nightmare of a dreamsong*
> *To the Chorus to sing!*
> *All other singers disturbed, the Ancestors fled*
> *His cursed song described a monster*
> *That would hunt those who bled!*
> *For the affront to our purpose*
> *He was left here to dream*
> *In hopes before he expired*
> *He be inspired by starlight, his spirit redeemed.*
>
> *Sharks! Sharks! He made the sharks!*
> *Not one dreamstar fell to the sea that night*
> *But instead a dark comet*

To bring rows of sharp teeth and source of great fright!
At the following Chorus, after many a year
All whales pooled their best dreams
To counteract the new fear.
The dreamt hopefuls were many
And the one that most stuck
Was of a clever kind with great power
But these turned out as ill luck.

Them! Them! The Black Cloaks with White Eyes!
They harried the sharks, but also took calves from the slow!
Dreams to even face darkness are tainted
The dreamers couldn't have known.
To make matters worse, at next Chorus, he appeared!
He sang of battle unending, how wounds never heal
For pure malice and destruction, he somehow persevered!
The wisened amongst us knew
His song needed no friend
So we lifted our voices in retaliation
And sang for an opposite end.

You! You! Precious babe of dreams!
Your kind was created, joining our kin
Those Who Cannot Be Unmarked
Savior to the many, absorbing his sin!
Then, last he came, he sang of fatal disease
United against it, we sang and sang hard
Reduced to minor illness, we denied the obscene!
Now look at each badge his own nightmares bring
Shark-bitten, degrading, covered in rot
Can he even survive singing another dark dream?
For the mercy of all, hopefully not.

Tahn's mind was awhirl with the harrowing story, tense, glancing between the advancing phantom of decay just below and her own flippers with their very few, yet undeniably permanent marks. Since the beginning of the Great Whale Spirit's dreaming—within which the earthly world, and the astral sea, and every other imaginable plane were believed to reside—all living things were supposed to be created by beautiful dreams in turn. It was quite discomfiting to be put aside from this, disconnected. She, her mother before her, and all others of her kind were not brought about by a dream desiring new and wonderful company like most whales, but because of...this? Not a bright, diamond-like falling star sent to scatter its promise into the ocean waves for the joy of tomorrow and generations to come, but rather a darkness shrunk down to a seedling, accompanied by only a breath of relief that it wasn't worse.

> *"Get ready!" the narwhal beside her cried.*
> *"He's bound to sing at any second!*
> *We must hold firm!*
> *Whatever it is, we must sing louder!*
> *All together, we have more power!"*

Over the increasingly restless, spiteful clicks and pipes of the unified, a group of sagely baleen whales with heavy ridges down their throats and impressively long, bumpy pectoral fins pointed them across the expanse at the isolated gathering of the Black Cloaks with White Eyes. They were the only kind not to join in the song of history, stoic and still, and these self-appointed wardens of their behavior threatened them in just a few shudderingly deep notes.

> *You*
> *Will*
> *Sing*

The accosted looked down and away, but no argument was made. The rest of the great Chorus eyed them untrustingly for only a glimpse, but Tahn's attention lingered. She felt a conflicted mote of kinship for them, having also been created in the course of a desperate plea instead of a sweet dream.

Then the decrepit whale stopped, arresting every heart in the congregation. His jaw hinged open, and from under patchy bristles once meant for filtering water from sustenance, a horrid column of inky darkness spewed up. The top of the dome scattered in a panic, swimming every which way to avoid being caught in the gush.

"Do your worst
You twisted thing!
You are nothing
But a reject of a dream!" the narwhal beside Tahn screamed.

The notes that ushered forth at last from the crackled body that was the target of the gathered's ire were long, trembling, and slow, but for nothing did they cease.

In my dream I see
The eclipse of everything
The loss of the sovereign empire sown
A force that reaps all that is known...

The crowd would tolerate no more. They heard the foretelling of an apocalypse and began their cries of dissent. Improvised songs of hope and everlasting light struck back against the tale of gloom from every packed portion of the ring of whales. Instead of a dance, they swam together with determined force in a circle around the corrupt central singer, containing and breaking apart the edges of the smoke that was trying to overwhelm their vision. Tahn did her best to keep up, lost in the crowd, unsure what to sing but a mantra of beautiful concepts—to hope, to love, to enliven—but the jittery, hostile motions that flickered within the shadows were deeply disturbing.

Their voices so overpowered the tune of the morose interloper that whatever else he sang, not a soul heard. At the end of his breath and will to stay afloat, the heaviness of his tainted body pulled him down, and he sank. Strength gave out, and he cared not how he tumbled in slow arcs once more into his own grimy clouds and the abyssal depths. The whole of whale-kind whistled and cheered when they saw, victorious laughter breaking out as they believed themselves free at last from the catastrophe-bringer and his horrid stench.

The swimming ring broke apart and dispersed as members of family pods sought each other for congratulations, but little Tahn merely allowed herself to be carried by the ebb and flow in their wakes. Her gaze was trained on the shadowy stranger, whose figure was shrinking rapidly into the astral sea's starry expanse. Soon, he would be swallowed entirely by his own personal current of darkness, possibly never to be seen again. And yet, as she observed him sinking, she saw resigned sadness rather than frustration or defeat. A squirm of pity unsettled her belly, far worse than anything in his ill appearance or the dark specters his dreamsong promised. Like her own, his song was unspun, not entirely heard. And to that point, it was really because of him that she came to exist in the first place. Tahn couldn't see her mother, she couldn't see any face she knew, and yet the one who fell below was someone she could not so easily let go.

Down she plunged, every sleek fiber of her being devoted to speed. She shimmied past everybody that came between her and her path, and not a single stranger she soared by caught on to her intention. Only those called the Black Cloaks with White Eyes noticed as she crossed the threshold from the Chorus into open space, her tiny body descending straight toward the corpse-like exile and his billowing smoke. They made not a sound nor gave away a single twitch of alarm, thoughts intuitively in agreement and kept to their own. Within their fraught time upon the world, they had never been sure of what to do that wouldn't be condemned, what to say that would not be twisted around. Whatever was happening with this little dolphin calf, whatever this meant, they felt the current of change was with her.

When Tahn released her held breath, she found that the other side of the choking inkiness was only more astral sea. Above, the blackness she forged through cleared. The congregation of whales was still tightly packed, but already so distant that it looked like a school of the tiniest fish. Below, she was grateful to see the exile had not vanished. Seemingly unconscious, he sunk ever further into the great expanse of dazzling celestial clouds, details obscured by so much color and distance. With no time to lose or doubt, the calf shot straight after him once more, hoping with all her tiny might to reach him before it was too late. A single question had awoken in her soul, and there would be no peace with anything she had learned or seen until it was solved.

She *must* ask, if there was any life left in him *to* ask.

The moment the great gathering fell beyond the reach of either eye or ear, a warning voice in Tahn's instincts arose, but she suppressed it. She careened through every cluster of twinkling dust, bursting right through the surface of astral rivers and hesitating for not even a blink in the wake of starry flames. The huge body of the banished one sank like lead through the cosmic landscape, falling faster and faster the further he got. Tahn pushed herself desperately in pursuit, not knowing where this chase would end, but only that she couldn't give up.

Hard as she tried, she could only force her small form to do so much, and in flagging for only a moment in a dense showering of miniature shooting stars, she lost him.

"Hello? Hello?
I'm sorry, but if you're there
Help me, I'm alone!"

Tahn, exhausted, called out many times in vain. At least, it seemed so at first. Just as she began to shudder and cry —wary, lonely, discovering regret—the stardust clouds gave way to a much more familiar, if not foreboding sight. Before her appeared a world of insulating cold, lit in deep blue and padded from beneath by piled sand. Dark, towering spires wavered into existence all around, forming stony arches between them. Their shapes were reminiscent of decayed coral, but on a giant scale, and as Tahn turned around to absorb the breadth of them, she discovered the body of the exile sprawled on the seafloor at their roots.

A single slow blink was the only movement he made, but it reassured her that he was alive. No bubbles arose from either of them, nor did she feel any lack of air to breathe, so Tahn imagined this must still be some part of the astral sea. It was a good thing too, because if this place were the true ocean, it would be much deeper than her mother ever allowed her to go as a fledgling.

"Excuse me
I'm Tahn.
And, who might you be?" she asked, floating down gently.

"Nuun," came the rumbling reply.

132

Black smoke leaked from the creases of his mouth and eyes with the effort of making the sound. He observed the tiny dolphin-kind briefly, complacently, and she returned the gaze with curious sympathy. Now was her chance.

> *"I am sorry to disturb*
> *But there is something that I need.*
> *They say there is beauty in every dream*
> *Something freed.*
> *But now I see that what they say*
> *Is not really what they mean.*
> *At the Chorus*
> *We sing the dream*
> *That is most beautiful to us.*
> *Now all I want to know that's true*
> *Is what's most beautiful in your dreams*
> *To you?"*

Nuun shifted his huge, calcified head and glanced out into the dark coral graveyard. It was a long moment, but he eventually closed his eyes and set into song. Plumes of both misty white and inky black swirled around him, kicked up by the tremoring notes and raspy clicks.

> *"To you I will tell the same as the rest*
> *Before they left me behind in the astral to sleep.*
> *Why did I delight, they asked*
> *In ruining a tradition held sacred*
> *Since every age that has passed?*
> *Because I was moved, profoundly*
> *By a vision of impenetrable fright.*
> *It was awe-inducing*
> *To be brought before my own life.*
> *Monumental, terrible*
> *Shatteringly beautiful."*

Tahn looked up at the mere hint of the distant sun's light high above, beyond the giant, lonely spires of twisted rock and far, far away from the real sea at all. She could only wonder at the sort of terrible fear Nuun described. It was difficult for her to reach within and churn up such a sensation from her limited memory, but its ominous head began to turn when she caught a glimpse of herself within her mind's eye. She was but a miniscule speck in this desolate place. So small, so very small, and so very far from her home, her mother, the Chorus...with naught for company but a corrupted exile who dreamt of horrors and death.

"Perhaps they were right
To always fight me," Nuun intoned laboriously.
"Maybe it is the nature of all living things
To smother whatever dark that they see.
Once I began down this path
I couldn't un-dream it.
I have slept for ages
Awaking only with the dreadful sights they'd omit.
I will be ended by this
But until the final omen takes wing and takes me
I cannot give up
On offering...the opportunity."

Tired, he fell silent, his song sputtering to a halt. Tahn observed him closely, compelled by his stillness and peace. He did not seem at all as malicious as the Chorus implied, and it confused her young heart. Though jitters crept in over what might lurk in the peripheral shadows, she steeled herself with the determination to form her own thoughts.

"I couldn't really hear your dreamsong before
I'm afraid.
Would you, maybe, for me, perform it once more?"

Nuun's vision recentered upon receiving such an unheard of request, a sliver of life returning to him yet. He heaved in a mighty breath of the dusky, oceanic air, and sang as distinguished a song as his deteriorated body would allow. Every deep, bellowing note shook the very substance of the astral sea where Tahn floated, close as she was.

In my dream I see
The eclipse of everything
The loss of the sovereign empire sown
A force that reaps all that is known.
The sudden shock
The suffocatingly slow
The lifetime of servitude
When freedom was once your own.
Changing irrevocably the world of water
And even worse the world of stone
With invisible tendrils
And weapons that are thrown.
So comes the destroyer
So comes what won't share
So ends all our time here
So begins that which won't care.

As Nuun keened this tragic soliloquy, Tahn caught a vision in the grime and sand that wafted up and drifted past her. Weak though it was without the support of the many in the Chorus, the astral sea still responded to the call of the dream. It looked like the silhouette of something reaching down toward the water's surface, obscured further by a crisscrossed mesh of fibers, only to draw its bizarre appendage back in disdain before the mirage disappeared.

"It does sound quite dreadful," the calf pondered.
"Is it something that's living?
Is it only us it would cull?"

Nuun's body groaned like a splintered tree submerged to such a depth that its entire husk was about to crack. He mustered a few tones with a cough of black ooze.

"I would not know.
What I see, I see from the view of our kind
This thing comes from above, and we live below."

Tahn watched his wheezing and the endless filaments that

departed from him with intense pity. Up close like this, she could see the dark trenches that cleaved through his flesh like those in the deepest reaches of the sea, swirling and curling all over in a way that wasn't entirely unbeautiful. He rested as if sleeping under her gaze, waiting so patiently for whatever the little calf could say. All she knew in that moment was that she wanted to say something that no one had ever said before, to try something no one had yet thought to try. She couldn't swim away now, she couldn't imagine trying to forget. It was too sad to even brush up against the thought of simply leaving him like this.

"I didn't get to finish my song to the stars either," she softly opined.

> *"Maybe we could sing together?*
> *Maybe a gift*
> *That is blended by two*
> *That sings of both pain and of joy*
> *Can bring something new?"*

The old whale roused to wakefulness once more, and he focused upon her truly for the first time since she arrived in his sleeping grave. A tug at the corner of his long, drawn mouth and a slow crease around the eye told Tahn his answer. She did a little twirl of happiness, then shut her own eyes and outstretched her flippers to conduct the song. Nuun's bassy tone ushered forth as she had hoped, trembling in rhythm to her lead.

This song was less specific, less bounded in its parts than either of the two dreams that inspired it, but a dreamsong nonetheless. Tahn's adulation of a cliffside lined with petal-filled trees and Nuun's lament of an all-powerful, all-consuming entity mixed into something uniquely bittersweet. At its highest high it was the song of holding that which is precious close, and at its lowest low it was a story of the loss that always comes at dream's end. It breathed life into a vision so vibrant that Tahn could see it perfectly behind closed lids.

In the dream she saw the sea, with the cliffside high above. With strange, yet dextrous appendages, the brand new being planted the saplings of her dearly wished for trees. All along the precipice and further down the inland slope, these brightly colored and fragrant saplings flourished, and the time finally came for them to burst with blossoms in the radiant season of spring. Then this wonderfully strange animal, and its children, and its children's children, gathered those petals that did not fall to the sea on their own in big shells and woven reeds, and brought them down to a beach with level shore. Here, they spun the stems into interlocking floral rings, and waded into the water to call out like a gull. They were greeted with fountain spouts and the excited squeaks of a family of playful sorts like Tahn's own kind, breaching to greet the world's newcomers. The beings of land, decorated with their flower crowns, reached out to place them as well on the beings of sea. The children of both kinds laughed and splashed, tossing petals and woven rings in games made for the day. The sunset would part them only for a time, for the great migrations would bring countless whale-kind by this coast, a joy shared for an age and, with hope, more to come.

When the vision finished and faded from her mind's eye, and the blended song completed its final notes, Tahn was excited to look to her forlorn friend and share in the wonder of their special creation, but...he was gone. His body lay lifeless on the sandy seabed, gray and barnacled, his jaw slack. There was no more sign of the tar that poured from him so incessantly before. The trenches and holes in his flesh were no longer oily or abyssal, but simple and matte, like scars accrued in an age past. But most startling of all was the appearance of an object Tahn could not understand. Protruding from Nuun's side was a rod of wood the length of a small whale itself, impossibly straight the whole way through. Where it stuck into his ribs was just the faintest gleam of silver, embedded deep within the hide. Tahn could not bring herself to look at it for too long, head hung in mourning for the fallen dreamer and too-quickly-lost friend. She had forgotten how his dreams afflicted him so severely, thinking their vision would be shared. She could only wonder at what he had seen.

Tahn breathed the true, earthly air with a gasp of relief. At some point in her swim toward the sun from Nuun's resting place, she found herself transported into real water and the real sea. With no sign beneath of the rocky spires or the shadow of the friend that had been, she had no choice but to carry on as swiftly as possible to the surface.

The horizon waves were tangerine, both in cloud and sea, the sky filled with puffy purples and the last of night's evenly spaced stars. This was indeed the world Tahn called home. Everywhere was water, and it carried the voice of her mother to her across the surf and through the currents. Tahn swam to her without delay, the promise of warm, loving nuzzles now the most wondrous dream she could possibly wish for.

When they found each other at last, there was much fussing and chattering squeaks. Many whales gathered near the heartwarming reunion and, together, all heads turned as flares of color in the sky signaled the arrival of the long awaited dreamsongs. The first to be freed from the heavens burst into a dazzling array high above the horizon. In the whizzing dance of sparks, all stars still visible in the early dawn light were pulled into a great whirlpool and thrown back out, scrambling them up into unique clusters and spread unevenly, as promised. Then the second one fell, spinning and throwing sparks as it dropped like a spherical diamond chunk. It splashed into the water of the horizon and threw up a giant spray in the shape of a tall, fronded tree with the enticing, hard-cased fruits its dreamer described.

Just when everyone was ready to cheer, expecting that to be the end of the Chorus's accomplishments this cycle, another star—unprecedentedly complex—began its descent. In the great arc it cut across the heavens, it was followed by a multiplicity of colored tails. Pulsing between a hollow dark and shimmering white at its center, it so dazzled its observers that they awed aloud, unable to consider yet if it were a sign of good or ill. Tahn was the most amazed of all, emotion overflowing as she recognized it in her heart. She watched it slowly careen beyond the horizon, flashing its light in a temporary farewell that she knew to be a promise. It may not be tomorrow, or even quite a few generations to come, but someday, when that dream came true, it would be very beautiful, in its own frightening, awe-inspiring, lovely way.

Biographies

Quill Holland

Quill Holland (he/him) is an author from New Zealand. Working as a programmer by day, Quill often writes at night. Growing up, he could always be found with his nose in a fantasy book or watching the latest science fiction movie. As a result, he's developed an imagination that never stops, and naturally, sci-fi and fantasy are primarily the domains that Quill's own work inhabits. When he's not debugging code or creating worlds, Quill likes to dabble in illustration and photography and explore the natural beauty of New Zealand with his partner. You can find Quill on his website: quillholland.nz.

Kay Koel

Kay Koel (she/her) lives and works in the United States and is currently polishing her first novel. She also collects hoodies, and haunts the streets of Saint Louis as a self-proclaimed coffee snob.

Amelia Lasser

Amelia Lasser (she/her) is a writer of short stories and graphic novels, and a curator of anthologies. When not writing, Amelia enjoys napping.

Trey Stone

Trey Stone (he/him) is the author of three novels and has made a habit out of writing dark and thrilling stories that don't pull any punches. He lives in Norway with his wife and enjoys heavy metal, mountain hiking, video games, decent Scotch, and great books. When he's not writing he can be found working at his day job as an archaeologist or daydreaming about his next tattoo.

Varya Kartishai

Varya Kartishai (she/her) is a 1st generation Philadelphia writer/artist whose work has appeared in Bewildering Stories and Page Bacon, and anthologies from After Dinner Conversation, B-Cubed Press and Ooligan Press. Some of her work can be viewed on Kindle and Goodreads.

Chris Romero

Christian "Chris" Romero (he/him) was born in Aruba to Colombian parents. He developed his two lifelong passions in early childhood: sport fishing and reading. He started penning his first book at the age of fourteen and promptly abandoned it forever. Then, he took up flash fiction and fan works on anonymous forums, earning positive feedback. Soon after, he moved to Colombia and pursued degrees in biology and microbiology, which gave him the chance to discover the breathtaking nature and customs of his parents' country. Living in such multicultural and diverse environments allowed him to meet people from many different backgrounds and discover their stories, which he aims to showcase and explore as imaginative fiction taking place in alternate realities.

Stephen Howard

Stephen Howard (he/him) is an English novelist and short story writer from Manchester, now living in Cheshire with his fiancée, Rachel, and their daughter, Flo. An English Literature & Creative Writing graduate from the OU, his work has been published by Lost Boys Press, Scribble, and Dark Recesses Press, among others.

Laki

Laki (they/them) is a mystery-loving, magic-obsessed forest creature from the foothills of California who somehow ended up with a BA in Film Studies after stumbling out of the trees for a minute. A sign outside of the cave Laki disappears into for months on end promises that if you leave snacks at the entrance, you will be thanked by having a little piece of your soul reflected in the next story or art piece that emerges in spring.

LOST BOYS PRESS

Like an intrepid ship's captain, Lost Boys Press is exploring new horizons, riding the high seas and interstellar winds of cutting edge science fiction and fantasy. We're committed to the powerful storytelling, the expression of self, and the breaking of conventions readers expect from the indie scene, nurturing bright new voices as we go.

Our mission is to bring the vibrancy and color of indie speculative fiction to as wide an audience as possible. In our books, you'll find tried-and-tested elements of science fiction and fantasy alongside genre-mashing, boundary-pushing, and occasional forays into history and creative non-fiction, especially where new stories can be told or expectations subverted.

We seek out imaginative speculative fiction with heart, hoping to show you things you haven't seen before and to leave you enriched when you turn the final page.

FIND OUT MORE

Head to our website to find our **indie bookstore**, where you can buy books and Lost Boys merch, and sign up to our **newsletter** to receive news, exclusive offers, and advance information on our upcoming releases!

WWW.LOSTBOYSPRESS.COM
SUPPORT INDIE

Find us on social media at 'lostboyspress.'